A HUMBUG HOLIDAY

FIREFLY JUNCTION COZY MYSTERY #4

LONDON LOVETT

WILD FOX PRESS

CHAPTER 1

"Why does it not surprise me to find my best friend in the donut shop on this chilly Tuesday morning?" Raine chirped from behind.

I pulled my focus from the fabulous trays of donuts, crullers and muffins long enough to greet her. She was wearing a red dress with a dark green knitted shawl dropped low over her shoulders. Silver bells dangled from her earrings.

"Hello. Someone is certainly in the holiday spirit," I quipped before turning back to the donut case. There were still three people ahead of me, so I had time to decide which donuts to pick for the office. It was my week and it was extremely important that I made wise choices.

Raine came up next to me to survey the treats too. "I'm feeling very merry. Just finished decorating my tree. It takes up half my living room. Now my entire house smells like a forest."

"I wish I could get into the spirit. Even with my mom coming to town, my money pit of a home is draining away my merriness. I didn't even bother with a tree. Ursula and Henry are still putting up crown moulding in the dining room. There's such chaos in the house, I'm just not in the mood to decorate."

"What a bah humbugger you are," Raine noted accurately. "Your sister has her place ready for a magazine shoot."

"I know. I figured I can never compete with Lana's incredible eye for perfection or Emily's knack for cozy country, so I just don't bother. Besides, I can go to their houses when I'm in the holiday mood."

"Nonsense. We need to get you in a permanently merry spirit. We'll walk through town for lunch today. They've started selling the goodies for the Firefly Junction Holiday Festival. The theme is Celebrating a Victorian Christmas. I've heard they're selling mincemeat pies and sugarplums. Whatever those are. We can't have you acting like a Scrooge all winter." Raine's tone hardened and her face drew into a scowl as she watched the woman in front of us buy up the last dozen green and red sprinkled cake donuts. "Hope you're proud of yourself, leaving the rest of us without any holiday sprinkled donuts," Raine snapped.

The woman turned around. "First come, first served," she said with a smirk.

"Donut hog," Raine muttered under her breath.

I leaned my head closer to her to lower my voice. "What was that about Scrooge and merry spirit?" I asked.

"I came here for the red and green sprinkled donuts," Raine complained.

"There are still plenty with the rainbow sprinkles." I pointed them out.

"Not the same. It's Christmastime. The red and green ones taste like a holiday treat. Rainbow sprinkles are for summer and birthdays."

I smiled at her. "And that's why I like you. Not many people have categorized donuts by season or celebration."

"Coffee latte for Aurora," the coffee barista called from the other end of the counter. A fit and trim woman carrying a black velvet top hat adorned with holly leaves and wearing a forest green blazer buttoned over riding breeches walked up to the counter to pick up her coffee. Her hair was tied neatly in a ponytail at the nape of her neck and she was wearing a sleek black pair of tall boots. Both the hairstyle and boots reminded me of Edward, who was at home, no doubt pouting in an upstairs room as Henry and Ursula pounded their '*blasted*' hammers against nails.

"I've always considered her an underappreciated Disney princess," Raine said lightly.

I looked at her. "That woman is a Disney princess?"

"No, don't be ridiculous. She's the woman running the horse-drawn carriage for the festival." Raine shook her head as if I was completely daft. "I'm talking about Aurora, the Disney princess from Sleeping Beauty. She's my favorite."

"Of course. Silly of me not to follow your odd train of thought. And I think Princess Rapunzel is the best with all that magical hair."

"Well, everyone is entitled to their opinion," Raine said with a chin lift.

The customers ahead of me had nearly cleared out the shelves. "I guess Tuesday is donut morning in this town." I finally reached the counter. My choices were limited now, which was probably a good thing. The young man working the counter filled the box for me. Raine ordered a maple cruller, and we walked out of the shop together.

School was out and the street was crowded with kids enjoying their freedom. The snow edged landscape vibrated with the excitement of the upcoming holidays. The town had started blasting Christmas carols from speakers set up around the shops. It seemed I was doomed to have Silver Bells and Rudolph stuck in my head for the next two weeks. A moment of nostalgia hit me as I watched three kids, dressed in beanies and puffy coats, drag a sled down the sidewalk and toward the end of town where several plump hills provided a perfect snowy playground for sleds and snowman building.

"Have you noticed that the princes all have a bigger part now? In fact some of them aren't even proper royalty, just off the street kind of guys, like Kristoff in Frozen." Raine posed the question and took a bite of cruller, keeping her hand beneath it to catch any falling shards of maple glaze.

"I see we're still talking about Disney. Yes, that's true. In the old movies like Sleeping Beauty, the prince was strictly eye candy. He had very little substance." We stopped at my jeep. "I don't know what's more disturbing," I said. "That we know so much about Disney movies, especially since neither of us have children or that we can actually spend time psychoanalyzing them."

A loud truck rumbled along the road. It was brimming with holly garland shaped like massive stars. "I was wondering when they were going to hang the stars on the streetlamps," Raine said. "I heard they had to delay it until the big tent was constructed for the holiday play. It's just not Christmas without those stars." As she spoke her earrings jangled.

I glanced down at my navy blue sweater and black pants. I really was starting to feel a little Scrooge-ish standing next to my holiday bedecked friend. "I suppose I should get more in the spirit. A walk to town is probably just what I need. But I'm not sure about mincemeat pie."

"Come on. Where's your Victorian sense of adventure?" Raine asked.

"I'm fairly certain Victorians weren't known for their sense of adventure. And it's less about the adventure and more about the idea of mixing meat and fruit together in a pie. But I'm happy to try sugarplums and whatever else they're selling at the festival."

"Great. Then we'll have you humming Christmas tunes in no time. By the way, when's your mom getting in?"

"Lana's picking her up at the airport in a few hours. I'm looking forward to her visit and her holiday stuffing. She makes the best."

Raine was halfway through her donut. "Lana said the same thing. I think she's looking forward to having your mom help out. She's managed to overbook herself for the holidays . . . as usual."

A police car rolled past following the crew that was about to hang the stars from lampposts.

"I better get to work before the police block off the streets." I unlocked the jeep. "And before my boss starts demanding his donut."

"Speaking of police," Raine said slyly. I knew exactly what would come next. Thus far, there was only a faint, unspoken thing happening between Brady Jackson, the town detective, and me. It was so faint, in fact, that it was basically invisible. "What has Firefly's most spectacular detective been up to and more importantly have the two of you kissed yet?"

"Sorry to leave you disappointed, my friend, but I don't know what he's up to at the moment. We've both been busy. I haven't heard from him in several weeks. And, no, there has not been a kiss. We've come close, but Jax decided the moment needed to be just right. We need a kaboom moment. And that just right moment has eluded us time and time again."

Raine shook her head in dismay. "Silly friend, a kiss from that man is the *kaboom* moment."

I laughed. "Hope so." As tempted as I was to add in that my nosy posy house ghost made sure the right time never happened, I was sworn to secrecy about my haunted inn. It was especially aggravating when I knew that, of all people, Raine would understand and be thrilled about it. "To be honest, I'm relieved that we haven't moved past a flirtatious friendship."

"Yes, of course you are," Raine said wryly.

"No, I mean it. I've suffered terrible heartbreak once. And my intuition tells me that handing my heart over to Brady Jackson would be equally dangerous. I don't want to go through anything like that again."

"Your ex-boyfriend, Brett, sounded like a real jerk. You were younger and not as savvy back then. You're a good match for Detective Jackson. Heaven knows someone has to rein in that man. He's been bouncing around as the town's most eligible bachelor for far too long. It's time he settles down."

I laughed. "I'll be sure to let him know that Raine thinks he should settle down. In the meantime, I've got to get these donuts to the office before Parker Seymour has a donut fit and decides to hand me the local grannies' knitting club for my next assignment."

Raine lifted her shawl higher to cover her shoulders. "Perfect. I need a lift back. I've got a card reading at nine." She hurried around the jeep and climbed into the passenger's side. "So lunch at noon?" she asked as I pulled away from the curb.

"Sounds good to me. Sometimes it feels like my work day is just a series of eating events connected by the occasional moments of writing."

CHAPTER 2

I'd spent far too long wasting time with Raine rather than fulfilling my important task of getting donuts to my editor. Parker burst out of his office, his thick moustache rocking back and forth like a fluffy bucking bronco, as I stepped inside with the precious pink box.

"Taylor, what took you so long? There had better be at least two maple bars in that box or you'll be stuck cold calling advertisers for the next two weeks," Parker grumbled.

Myrna looked up from her computer with anticipation. She was the one usually stuck with the odious task of selling ad spots for the paper.

I smiled sweetly at her and lifted the box lid. "Three maple bars and a maple cruller, just in case." Parker marched over so hard, his big feet sent tremors across the floor. The old flyers and articles pinned to the wall fluttered in the breeze he created. He reached into the box and grabbed out two maple bars.

"Guess you dodged a bullet," he muttered before returning to his office and swinging shut the door.

Myrna's enthusiastic posture deflated. "Darn it. Oh well, nothing can ruin my morning." She reached under her desk and pulled out a large, round hat box decorated with green ribbon. "My festival bonnet arrived this morning." Myrna pulled on her bright red velvet bonnet and tied the big satin bow on the side of her chin. The front edge was trimmed with white faux fur, and the lining was a satiny tartan plaid.

Myrna held out her arms and turned her head side to side. "What do you think?"

"It's gorgeous. It goes so perfectly with your dark hair and that new red lipstick you're wearing." I carried the donuts over to her desk.

She waved her hand as if I'd brought her a box of vipers. "No, no. I've got the holiday dance recital in less than a week, and the costume is still a size too small. I've got to avoid anything with sugar, or butter . . . or calories, for that matter."

I closed the box tightly to seal away the tempting aroma. "I'm sure they aren't that tasty anyhow. They look kind of greasy today." Myrna had taken up dancing at my suggestion, and it had turned into her full-time hobby. I wanted to support her in any possible way.

"You do realize that *greasy* only makes them sound more tempting," Myrna said with a laugh. She pulled out a hard candy. "It's sugar free." She stuck it in her mouth and got back to work still wearing the bonnet.

The front door swung open thrusting a cold swoosh of air across the papers on Myrna's desk. She smacked them all down as if playing the Whack-a-mole game.

"You too, with the fancy hat?" Chase chided as he strode past us. "Rebecca just spent a fortune on an entire custom made Victorian dress and matching bonnet. She looks beautiful in it, of course, but it's still a lot of money for a few days of a street festival." Chase, our lead reporter, was solidly back with his girlfriend, Rebecca

Newsom. Conveniently enough for Chase, her father owned the *Junction Times*. It was a great way to ensure job security. Although, I imagined it was equally stressful.

The hard candy crunched between Myrna's teeth and she swallowed. "Not all of us can afford to have the entire outfit. I'm happy with my bonnet, and I bought a matching white fur muff. What are you wearing to the festival, Sunni?"

I was in the process of plucking out a jelly donut when she asked the question. I blinked in response. "Wearing? I didn't know a costume was required."

"Well, it's not." Myrna looked pointedly at my drab desk. "I suppose it depends on your level of spirit." She had spruced up her desk with a green garland dotted with gold bows and silver bells. A vintage Santa Claus was sitting on the corner of her desk, cheerily smiling down at her pile of papers. Even Chase had taken the time to add a teensy live Christmas tree to his work area. The only things on my desk were a stapler, a container of pens and yesterday's coffee cup.

I looked back at Myrna. "This is the second time this morning I've been scolded for lacking holiday cheer. And yet, I'm not moved to spend any money on a bonnet or a muff or jingle bell earrings. I've got way too many money sucking projects at the inn." I tromped out of the room with my box of donuts and placed them in the lunch lounge.

"Taylor, get in here!" Parker's voice boomed through the office causing my shoulders to jerk up around my ears. I left the box on the table and hurried to my desk for my notebook and pen.

Parker was sitting behind his desk shoving the tip of a nasal spray into a nostril. He waved to the empty chair with his free hand, a movement that sent three of his sticky notes off his computer and onto his desk. He finished spraying his nose and swept the runaway sticky notes off the manila folder sitting in front of him. I was certain I read a note reminding him to buy his wife a Christmas present, which I found humorous enough that a smile popped up.

"What are you so cheery about?" he grumbled. "The only thing worse than cold weather is cold weather during the holidays. The frigid temperatures zap your immunity just before you have to heave yourself into crowded shopping malls and parties that are ripe with germs." For a man who spent much of his day worrying about his health, Parker rarely ever had a cold or flu. That might have been due to the gallons of hand sanitizer he used.

"Yeah, I know I sound like Scrooge," he said, even though I hadn't said one word.

"No, you're right," I sat forward, which caused him to instinctively lean back and away from my possible germs. "When I was a kid, I distinctly remember always spending at least three or four of my winter break days in bed with a cold. And this morning, it's been alluded to more than once that I, too, am a Scrooge. So, I guess misery loves company, or in our case, miserable people love company." I laughed lightly, hoping he'd find my comments funny. Instead, he just wriggled his red nose at me as if I was babbling a lot of nonsense. Which I was.

"Then this assignment is right up your alley." Parker picked up the manila folder and tossed it my direction. "A group of business folk always put on a holiday play for the festival. It's usually boring and chaotic. I'm sure this year will be no different. But the local businesses are our bread and butter," he said for the millionth time since I'd started working at the newspaper. The *Junction Times* was a small paper, but some of my articles had helped it gain more of a readership. I was proud of that fact. Parker was too, only I'd learned early on that he wasn't the type of editor to heap praise on anyone.

"Scottie Sherman is your contact," Parker continued. "She's the drama teacher at Smithville High. She's in charge of this year's production of *A Christmas Carol*."

I looked up from the folder in my hand. "You mean the Scrooge story?"

"Is there any other?" Parker asked as he dragged a box of throat lozenges out of his desk drawer.

"I'm covering the production of the play?" My tone told him exactly how uninspired I was by my new assignment.

"Yes. Interview the cast members and make sure to give a little shout out to their various businesses in the article. That kind of free advertisement is the reason they sign up to do the play. Hopefully, it will be enough to bring them around for some actual paid ad space in the paper."

"In other words, write a glowing piece about the local production of *A Christmas Carol* and hope it translates to some advertising money," I said wryly.

"Exactly. Now go out there and get the scoop. Just don't bring back any germs when you return to the office." He dropped the lozenge into his mouth and waved me out with his hand.

CHAPTER 3

*S*cottie Sherman, the woman in charge of the play, picked up on the first ring. "Sherman here. If you're calling to tell me you can't make dress rehearsal, then I'll find a replacement. That's my rule. Dress rehearsal or done," she said, short and to the point, in true high school teacher fashion.

"Actually, I'm not in the play. My name is Sunni Taylor and I work for the *Junction Times*."

"Oh yes, I read your column all the time. The only thing in that scrappy paper worth reading."

My face warmed at the compliment. I liked her already. "Thank you so much. That's nice to hear. My next assignment is an article on the holiday play."

A short laugh shot through the phone. "An article? You mean the free advertising bribe for the actors? Don't get me wrong, I'm thrilled to have so many fine *thespians*." She cleared her throat loudly in case I didn't catch the sarcasm. "It's only that I know the motive of the cast members has more to do with their business than with entertainment. Some of them are not much better than my students when it comes to attention span and enthusiasm. And yet, I volunteer for this play every year." It seemed I'd caught her at a bad moment. "I torture myself with this every year when I should be sitting at home by the fire, binge watching all the shows I'm too tired to watch during the school year. That's what the rest of the staff is doing, but no, I'm out here covered in glitter because the two high school students who volunteered to work on set and props decided not to show up." She finally took a breath. "But you don't need to hear all this." Her tone lightened. "I'll be here all morning working on set decorations. Come by anytime. I'm happy to answer questions."

"Thank you. I was just heading out right now. Is this morning all right?"

"Sure. You can't miss me. I'm wearing a pair of felt reindeer antlers on my headband."

"Perfect. I will keep an eye out for antlers."

After my declaration that I wouldn't be joining in on the Victorian fashion show, Myrna had been unusually silent the rest of the morning. She managed to scowl my direction a few times as well. It seemed like a perfect morning to get out of the office. It would be my first tour of the festival.

A chilly snap froze my cheeks and nose as I walked along Edgewood Drive toward the center of activities. I pulled the collar of my winter coat up and shrank my head down like a turtle, trying to shield myself from the cold. Drifts of sooty colored snow lined the curbs, and puddles of melted ice dotted the sidewalk and street. Two mounted policemen rode by on their trusty four-legged partners. One of the officers had added red ribbon to his horse's bridle. A green sprig of holly fluttered on the band of his hat as he politely nodded at me. Even the policemen were more festive than I was.

The town had pulled out all the stops for the festival. The city workers were halfway through with the task of hanging Raine's beloved stars on the streetlamps. Every shopfront was draped in twinkling lights. Festoons of evergreens and red berries framed windows and doors, mimicking the common holiday decor of the nineteenth century. The large wrought iron gazebo in the park at the end of town was nearly obliterated by pine tree branches heavily coated with silvery white flocking. A circle of bright green music stands decorated with tartan bows had been arranged in front of the town hall. A hand-painted sign framed in glittery snowflakes listing the hours when visitors could enjoy the caroling group stood next to the music stands.

I strolled past the city hall. A small patch of green, adjacent to the city building, was being set up with a Nativity scene. A few people had gathered to watch the manger being filled with three impressively crafted wise men. A woman, thirty-something with curly brown hair and round hazel eyes that looked red from either crying or allergies, was arranging pale yellow straw around the wooden cradle. She paused her task to pull two pieces of straw out of her bright blue sweater. The sweater was covered in white satin snowflakes that looked as if they'd been cut and hand sewn onto the garment. Where on earth did people find the time? The woman lifted her face briefly. I quickly washed away the idea that the straw was causing her allergies. It was obvious she was distraught about something. I doubted it had anything to do with the way the straw was placed.

I walked past the booth that was boasting 'sweet treats' and the 'most mouthwatering sugarplums in town'. I'd venture to say they were also, most likely, the only sugarplums in town. Someone had taken the time to paint a delightful army of nutcrackers across the large banner on the booth. Iced gingerbread men, raspberry and chocolate thumbprint cookies and chocolate glazed cream puffs filled the trays. A triple layer white porcelain cake stand stood proudly in one corner of the booth stacked heavily with round cookies that had been covered with a metallic purple glaze. A gold sign beneath the cake stand announced that sugarplums cost two dollars each. I had no idea what ingredients were tucked into a Victorian sugarplum, but I was certain the originals were not coated in metallic purple. Aside from the modernized sugarplums and, I suspected, the far from accurate mincemeat pies, the rest of the festival food was just what one could expect at a street fair. A massive char covered barbecue had been set with spits of tri-trip, and a stand dedicated solely to every kid's favorite vegetable, corn on the cob, boasted ten different toppings ranging from parmesan cheese to a secret holiday spice mix. Hot cider and hot cocoa were being served from under a red and white canvas pop-up tent. The line for hot drinks was already curled around the corner.

On my way toward the giant white tent, the venue for the play, I scooted closer to the mincemeat pie booth. I had to admit, the golden flaky crusts and buttery aroma drifting from the hot pies made my mouth water. Maybe I would have to venture toward a Victorian style lunch after all.

I stepped inside the large event tent. Its panels fluttered with the breeze outside, but the canvas did an impressive job of keeping out the chill. In fact, the atmosphere inside the tent was almost humid and warm. Large pieces of cardboard were half finished with fantastical scenes of Charles Dickens' London. One particularly wonderful display was the interior of a shop, Scrooge's shop, no doubt. The diamond shaped panes of the leaded glass windows were gray with soot but revealed a snowy scene outside. A single, half melted candle stood in the center of a wooden table. Stacks of gold coins surrounded the candle. The fire in the hearth behind the table was a small, sputtering flame.

As I perused the richly painted backdrops, a pair of felt reindeer antlers popped out from behind a scene of the village. A pair of blue eyes followed. "You must be Sunni." Scottie stepped out from behind the cardboard prop. She was holding a clipboard, and I half expected to see a whistle hanging from a string around her neck. But it seemed Scottie had left her teacher's whistle behind and replaced her neck ware with a necklace strung with tiny blinking Christmas lights. She was wearing round glasses with candy cane striped frames.

Scottie's mouth pursed slightly as she took in my very non-holiday outfit. I wondered just how many other people I'd offend throughout the day with my lack of spirit.

I gazed up at the painted backdrops. "Your sets are amazing. I feel like I'm standing in nineteenth century England. Did you draw them all yourself?"

"I wish I had that kind of talent. The advanced art class drew everything. Unfortunately, they ran out of time before school let out. As I mentioned in my long winded rant, the two students who were supposed to help, never showed. I've just been painting them." She held up her free hand to show the red and brown paint for proof. "I apologize, by the way."

"For what?" I followed her to a table where she had paints and brushes lined up on sheets of butcher paper.

"For filling your ear with my complaints. You called right after one of the actors, the Ghost of Christmas Present, called to say he'd be late to dress rehearsal. It's so hard to get everyone's schedule lined up for rehearsal, so every little change of plans causes a big domino effect." She lifted the clipboard and lightly tapped her mouth. "There I go again whining and complaining to you." She set down her clipboard.

"Truly, I don't mind. I can only imagine what a monumental task it must be to bring together an entire holiday play and with private citizens, no less. At least at school the students are right there, a sort of captive cast."

"And ones that have an incentive, the threat of a grade hanging over their heads. Drama class counts just as much as the other classes when it comes to calculating grade point average." She picked up a can of black paint. "If you don't mind, I'm going to outline the thatch roofs on the cottages while we talk."

"Absolutely. I don't want to get in your way. If there are any cast members available, I could start with their interviews, so you can finish your work."

Scottie adjusted the antlers on her thick blonde hair. "I'm afraid they are all still at work. They'll be here later this afternoon. I'm sure you'll get lots of information from them. Unfortunately, most of it will be about their businesses and not much about the play."

I pulled out my phone and followed her to the cardboard sets. "Do you mind if I record our conversation? I normally bring a notepad and pen but my hands get too cold in this weather to write quickly. Then my notes look like an abstract collection of scribbles."

Scottie stopped in front of the first cottage in the village scene. "I don't mind. I'm afraid I don't have too many exciting details to share. I chose *A Christmas Carol* this year because I knew it fit in with the Victorian theme the town council had chosen for the festival. We're doing a very pared down version of the original, of course." She paused to draw her paint covered brush along the edge of the cottage roof. "I'm afraid an hour is about max for audience attention span these days."

I held the phone up to catch the conversation. "You mentioned the cast members are local business owners?" I said it as a question, hoping she'd fill in some details.

"Yes, all from various businesses ranging from pizza restaurants to gift boutiques to dry cleaning. Then, of course, there are several local real estate agents. They almost always volunteer. In fact, Scrooge will be played by Evan Weezer, the number one agent in the state."

"Yes, I've seen his name on a number of signs," I noted. "Other than the logistics of various schedules, what is the biggest obstacle to pulling off a successful show?"

Scottie laughed. "How long do you have?"

I smiled. "Maybe just a few of the more trying problems. I know you mentioned trying to get everyone on the same page as far as scheduling."

"Yes, what's the phrase? Like herding cats." Scottie dipped the brush into the black paint. She turned to the backdrop and black paint dripped on the snow covered tree sitting next to the cottage. "Darn it." She pulled out a cloth and quickly wiped the drips away.

"Scottie, you're so busy. I feel I'm in the way. I'll come back later when the cast members are around and try and get a few statements without getting in the way of your production."

"Are you sure? I really don't mind answering questions." She pulled the brush away from the cardboard and managed to smudge her forehead with black paint as she reached up to adjust her antlers. She blinked at me. "I just painted my forehead black, didn't I?"

I nodded. "I could get it if you have some clean cloth."

Scottie waved off my offer. "No, I might as well wait until I'm finished and then stand under a hot shower to hose down. After all, I'm a teacher. I can't count how many times I've gone through an entire day with a streak of black permanent marker on my face without knowing it. In elementary school the sweeties are quick to let you know, but in high school it's comedy gold to let the poor kooky teacher walk around with it all day."

I laughed. "I suppose that would be comedy gold."

"Maybe it would be better if you come back later. If that's all right. I'm sure you're more interested in the cast member interviews anyhow. They are the stars, after all," she said with a smirk.

"Looking at all you've done here so far and with what appears to be little help, I'd say you are definitely the star of this production."

My compliment pleased her. "That's nice of you to say. Come back whenever you like, and we'll make time for you."

"Great. I'm coming back here for lunch. I'll drop by after I sample the Victorian treats."

"Don't bother with the sugarplums." She pushed the brush back into the paint. "They're just sugar cookie balls covered with an artificially sweet glaze. But the mincemeat pies are delicious."

"Thanks for the tip. I'll see you later." My phone rang as I headed out of the tent. It was Lana.

"Hey, Lana, did Mom get in O.K.?"

There was a short pause. "Why, yes, she did as a matter of fact." Another short pause. "She brought along a friend." Lana was speaking in an unusually hushed tone, the opposite of her usual voice.

"Why are you nearly whispering? Who did she bring? Oh my gosh, is it her bingo partner, Wanda? She never stops talking."

"No, no it's not Wanda."

"Is that Sunni?" Mom called from what sounded like another room. "Tell her to come by. I want her to meet Chris."

"Did she just say Chris?" I asked.

"Yes, yes she did." Lana's teasing tone was starting to annoy me.

"Chris as in Christina, her book club friend?" I asked.

"Nope," Lana said succinctly. "Chris as in Christopher, her new boyfriend."

My foot landed directly in a mound of slushy snow, and I nearly slipped onto my bottom. My phone fell, but with quick reflexes, I caught it before it, too, landed in the pile of snow. "Ah ha, got it," I said triumphantly as if I'd just caught the homerun at a softball game. "You just missed my catch. I've still got lightning reflexes," I bragged into the phone. "Back to the conversation," I laughed, although it sounded more like a twitter. "I almost thought I heard you say that mom brought her new boyfriend along for the visit."

"You didn't *almost* hear it. That's exactly what I said."

I froze to the spot on the sidewalk and quickly tried to sort out my feelings, but they were way too jumbled and just a touch too cold.

"You should come by this morning," Lana said. It wasn't a suggestion but more of a plea.

"I'll be there in twenty minutes."

CHAPTER 4

'd gone over and over in my head how I'd greet this supposed boyfriend, the man who mistakenly thought he could step into my dad's shoes. Every scenario sounded rude in my mind. We all adored Pops, and he was crazy-nuts about my mom. My brother was never too into team sports but I loved them. I was the competitive athlete in the family, so I always secretly considered myself Pops' favorite. We were extremely close. His loss was like having all the connective threads in my life cut at once. Emily and Lana were closer with Mom, but for me, it was always Pops. I knew it was ridiculous and totally immature, but I couldn't help feeling like Mom was betraying Pops by dating another man.

Lana heard my jeep and came bounding out onto the front porch to get a few secretive comments in before we stepped inside. She grabbed my arm and leaned closer. "He's very nice and not exactly Clark Gable, but Mom seems happy so try and keep it together."

"What are you expecting from me, a full on temper tantrum?" I whispered loudly.

"Judging from the tone of that whisper, yes, possibly. I know how you feel about Pops' memory, but just be open minded. Mom still has a long life in front of her."

"Enough with the big sister lecture." I straightened my sweater and cleared my throat as if I was going into a job interview. "Let's get this over with."

"That's the spirit," Lana chirped and then rethought her assessment. "Sort of."

We walked inside. Mom's laugh floated out from the kitchen. I knew all her laughs, and this was definitely her extra feminine and charming laugh. She always used it when trying to get an extra nice cut of beef from Jeb, the butcher, a grizzled old sailor with leathery skin and a salty, rough voice who had a bit of a thing for my mom.

My mom's travel friend, Chris, as it were, pushed politely up from the sofa as Lana and I entered the living room. He was short with a small paunch that hung over his belt. A bald spot seemed to be taking over most of his head, but I had to admit (as much as I hated to) he had a very nice smile.

Mom hopped up and rushed over for a hug. "It's my favorite ray of *sunshine*," she gushed as she threw her arms around me. Mom had taken to wearing her hair in a short, modern bob cut where the front was longer than the back. She sent each of us about a dozen pictures of the haircut before she decided to go for it. At the time, I thought it was strange for her to go so contemporary and stylish, but it seemed she was setting her sights on a wider social circle, one that included a man. She was wearing her favorite Santa earrings and matching necklace, the sight of which sent a streak of nostalgia through me. Thinking about Christmas morning around the tree, playing with our toys, and Mom bedecked in her Santa jewelry and reindeer printed apron for making Christmas dinner helped wipe away some of the negative aura I'd carried into the house.

"It's good to see you too, Mom." I forced a smile at her friend.

He walked hesitantly forward to shake my hand. I wondered briefly if Mom had filled Chris in on the exact reactions he could expect from each daughter. I was sure she'd warned him that I would be the path of most resistance. That sent a cold weight to the bottom of my stomach. I was going to have to give the man a chance.

"So nice to meet you, Sunni." His voice was sort of thin and quiet for a man. But there was nothing wrong with a soft spoken man, I quickly reminded myself. "I understand you're the reason your Mom's den is filled with trophies and ribbons," he said with a wink at Mom.

He's been in the den? What other parts of Pops' house has he sat in? Ugh, be gone negativity. I was taking my Scrooge role to new heights today. "Yes, I guess most of them are mine." I grinned Lana's direction. She looked sort of stiff and tight jawed as if she worried I wasn't going to, as she so nicely put it, keep myself together. "There *is* one small trophy on the shelf that Lana won for best handwriting at Sycamore Elementary School."

"And I'm quite proud of it," Lana piped up. "I'll go into the kitchen and put on a pot of coffee." She loosened her posture, seemingly convinced I was going to remain civil. Which, of course, I had every intention of doing, but my sister was a worry wart. "Sunni, why don't you come in and help me," she added. Maybe she wasn't convinced after all.

"Nonsense, Lana," Mom said. "Let Sunni stay here so we can catch up. I've already heard all about your business in the car ride home. I'd like to hear how Sunni's doing with her newspaper job and the Cider Ridge Inn."

I flashed a wide cheeked smile at my sister and took a seat in the big upholstered arm chair next to the couch. I hadn't had much time to visit Lana in the past week since she'd put the finishing touches on her holiday decor. Naturally, she had outdone herself. A tall spruce tree was nestled near the rustic brick hearth in the living room. Every inch of the tree was covered in thick silver and red garland, twinkling gold lights and hand painted glass ornaments. A lush evergreen garland with the same lights and ornaments was draped along the mantel, and a large green and gold wreath with red velvet bows hung over the fireplace. There were even leafy swags of greenery hanging over the various doorways in the house.

"Lana did such a wonderful job decorating," Mom said. "I can't wait to see what Emi has done to her place." She didn't bother mentioning seeing my house because she knew me too well. I might have won the trophies, but my sisters won when it came to interior decorating and making things beautiful. Mom folded her hands primly in her lap. "So how is your job at the paper?"

"Your mom is very proud of your journalism career," Chris said with a smile that added a few lines to his cheeks. "I've read some of your columns. You are very talented."

It seemed Mom's new friend was working hard to earn my approval. Was it already that serious that he was looking for kid approval? I pushed the silliness from my head. "Thank you. That's very kind of you, but I'm still always learning."

"Aren't we all," he chuckled. "I'm constantly having to keep up with new technology at my job."

"Chris is an electrician," Mom interjected.

"An electrician? How interesting." I glanced pointedly at Mom. Pops was a proud plumber. He always considered electricians to be arrogant know-it-alls. His narrow opinion had come from working on many construction sites where plumbers and electricians had to work side by side. Mom knew exactly why I looked her direction, but she chose not to make eye contact on the subject.

The rich aroma of coffee preceded my sister's light footsteps into the living room. "Emi made some apple crisp. If you're hungry, Mom, Chris, we can heat some up now."

Chris got up to help her carry the tray to the coffee table. "It sounds delicious and your mom has told me Emily is a great baker. But I can wait until later. We had breakfast on the plane."

Lana's phone buzzed from the kitchen. "Oops, left my phone behind." She headed toward the kitchen to retrieve her phone, leaving me alone with the *couple* again. I had to admit, Mom looked very happy.

"Where did you two meet?" I asked.

They both started to talk, but Chris politely bowed out and let Mom tell the story. "It was rather funny actually. I was in the grocery store at the refrigerator section trying to decide what flavor of yogurt to buy when a very nice voice behind me said 'try the key lime, it's delicious.'" Mom paused to take a sip of from her cup. I waited for her to continue, figuring the humorous part of the story was just around the bend. She lowered the cup to the saucer and smiled.

"Oh, was that it?" I asked. "I take it that Chris was the one telling you to try key lime."

"Yes, of course. He has a very nice voice. And he was right. The key lime yogurt was delicious."

Chris stared down at his cup, seeming a little embarrassed that the story of their meeting didn't quite live up to a rather funny story. His face popped up. His eyes had a nice warm glow. "And we've been giving each other yogurt suggestions ever since. We might even move on to ice cream recommendations soon, when things get more serious."

I laughed at his comment, which caused my mom to wink at him as if to say good job, you might just win her over

Lana was just hanging up from a call when she walked back

into the room. Her face looked decidedly more droopy than when she'd walked out.

"What's the matter, Lana?" Mom asked. "You look upset."

"Just a little business let down. A big wedding reception I have scheduled for January just fell through. Apparently, the groom got cold feet. I've already purchased some of the decorations and table linens."

"That's a shame. Will you be out a lot of money?" Mom asked.

"Fortunately, I always collect a good deposit before I start purchasing supplies. And it's non-refundable at this late date." Lana picked up a cup of coffee from the tray and sat on the opposite arm chair.

"That's smart business sense," Chris said. "It's always good to get some sort of deposit first."

"Yes, but I'm always disappointed when I lose a big event, and this one was going to have three hundred guests."

"Wow, impressive," Chris added. He was working the whole room and doing a good job.

Mom seemed to think so too as she settled proudly back against the seat cushion. "There'll be plenty more jobs, Lana. People are always getting married." She looked pointedly at each of us. "Well, most people." She seemingly forgot about the genteel, refined persona she'd been using around her new boyfriend and allowed her natural mom sarcasm to slip out.

"Anyhow," Lana said with some force, "the bride-to-be sounded pretty distraught. Poor thing. I think she was paying for a lot of it herself. I haven't met the groom. He had no particular interest in the wedding planning."

"He sounds like a toad," Chris said plainly. Lana and I had a good snicker. He'd gotten two laughs out of me in one sitting. Not too bad.

"Well, I've got to stop by the inn and check on—check on things." Yet again, I came dangerously close to mentioning my ghostly tenant. Henry and Ursula had been working in the dining room since seven. I was certain the noise would have Edward tense and grumpy.

Chris and Mom stood up to see me out. "How is the inn coming?" Mom asked. "I'm anxious to see the progress." She looked at Chris. "You should have seen how dilapidated that old place was when she first moved in."

"Actually," I said with a glance toward Lana, who was holding back a grin, "Chris, you'll be able to see it in all its dilapidated glory after all. Progress on the remodel is slow and expensive."

"I'll bet," Chris said. "Old houses like that generally need a lot of electrical work as well."

"Yes, I'm happy to say I have that hurdle jumped already. I decided to update the wiring before digging into any more of the interior."

"Smart girl," Chris said.

I hugged Mom at the door. An awkward moment followed where it seemed Chris and I were expected to hug. We shook hands. Mom looked disappointed.

"Don't forget, Sunni," Lana said. "We're all meeting at Emi's for dinner."

"I haven't forgotten. See everyone then but now journalism duty calls. I'm interviewing the cast for the annual Christmas play. Yet another important assignment," I chirruped as I headed out the door.

CHAPTER 5

I never knew if it was a good sign or a bad sign when Edward didn't make an instant appearance as I stepped into the house. As usual, Ursula was berating her brother, Henry, for doing something wrong. Although, most of the time it was nothing more than a bent nail head or placing the ladder at the wrong spot on the floor. After months with the two of them traipsing around the house, hammering, sawing and arguing with each other, I'd learned to ignore Ursula's incessant harping. Just like her brother, Henry.

My dogs, Redford and Newman, were napping peacefully in the kitchen. They'd also learned to ignore Ursula's shrill lectures. My footsteps startled them out of their naps. Both dogs bounded toward me for a hug and treat.

"Hello," I called into the empty kitchen. "Anyone home? And by anyone I mean any unhappy spirits?" I said with a weak laugh. No response. I headed out of the kitchen to check in on Ursula and Henry. A cold swoosh of air fluttered through my hair from behind as I stepped into the hallway.

"I'll soon go mad from the racket. Then you'll not only have a dead Englishman but a *mad* dead Englishman lingering in your house." I spun around. Edward was leaning against the edge of the kitchen table with his loose, rumpled cravat, shiny black boots and scowling expression. "And I don't mean *mad* in the angry sense like you modern people use. I mean it in the daft, lunatic sort of way."

"Yes, thank you. I got that from the context."

"I don't know what this means—from the context."

"Not important." I stepped back into the kitchen. Newman was already at Edward's feet with a tennis ball jammed between his teeth. I couldn't tell a soul about Edward, but my two dogs not only knew he existed, they'd both come to adore him. The fact that he could ricochet a tennis ball off three walls with one throw certainly helped his status.

"What will you do about it?" he asked.

"Nothing. It needs to get done. Or do you want the inn to be declared uninhabitable so that the city can tear it down?"

"It's perfectly inhabitable," he insisted. The ping of a hammer echoed down the hallway causing Edward's image to tighten with tension.

"Look, I'm sorry that you have to put up with so much noise. I'm sure after years and years alone in this house, it's a dramatic change. Trust me, this, you included, is a dramatic change for me too. We just have to forge ahead and look for the bright side of things."

Ursula screeched something at Henry in between hammer blows. It was an ill-timed disruption considering my quick pep talk.

"And what would the bright side of that clamor be?" Edward asked. "I suppose I should consider myself lucky that she's only here from sun up to sun down and not through all hours of the night."

I smiled. "See, you found a bright side."

His dark brow arched. "I assure you it was not intentional." He surveyed me from head to toe. "Where are you going dressed in that drab attire?"

"Back to work and it's not drab, it's professional. I'm doing a story on the Firefly Junction Festival play."

"Riveting," he drawled and plucked the tennis ball from Newman's teeth. With incredible, otherworldly precision, he managed to throw the ball down the hall so it would bounce into the dining room where they were working.

Newman tore after it. Seconds later, Ursula yelled at the dog for playing ball in the house.

Newman came plodding back, ball in teeth and tail between his legs. I tilted my head and stared at Edward.

He shrugged his broad, transparent shoulders. "What can I say? I have a talent for throwing."

"And a talent for upsetting Ursula, which, in turn, makes her yell and fuss, which, in turn, makes you angrier, or as you say, mad. It would probably help things considerably if you stopped harassing her."

"Harassing," he repeated in his annoying impression of my American accent. He made extra sure to flatten the middle letter *a*, which gave extra emphasis to the middle syllable 'ass'. "You use this word about me often. It no doubt means something unfavorable."

"There you go—that's what 'from the context' means," I said, satisfied that at least one positive had come from my side trip home.

"Who are you talking to, Sunni?" Henry's voice came from behind. He glanced around the room and saw both dogs sitting next to the kitchen table. What he didn't see was the focus of their attention. "Talking to those dogs again, eh?"

"Yes, I know, I'm nutty." I was constantly using the dogs as an excuse for talking to *myself*. At least this time they were sitting close enough for it to be plausible.

"Not at all. I used to have a parakeet that I talked to all the time. He was a way better listener than Ursula. But I'm sure a rock would be a better listener than my sister."

"Indeed," Edward drawled. His image disappeared completely as Henry made his way to the refrigerator. "Just need a cold drink. I've worked up a thirst with that hammer. The room should be all ready for a Christmas tree by tomorrow," he said into the fridge. He emerged with a can of soda and popped it open.

"I'm sorry—what Christmas tree?" I asked.

His expression flattened. "Well, your holiday tree, of course. Aren't you planning on putting one up? Ursula and I put ours up two weeks ago. I told her it was far too early and that it would be just a trunk full of kindling by the time Christmas arrived, but you know how well she listens."

"Yes, the rock comparison is still fresh." I decided a cold bottle of tea might give me a new burst of enthusiasm for the work day. I walked past Henry to the refrigerator. "I'll probably just skip a tree this year, Henry. My sisters have their houses decorated—"

"Skip the tree?" Ursula said sharply as she entered the kitchen.

Edward had vanished when Henry entered, but I didn't need to see him to know Ursula's arrival had sent him straight up to the second floor, to the farthest room in the house, most likely. Before she continued on her no tree tirade, she took the time to lecture Henry. Her hands went on her tiny hips. They got lost in the folds of denim fabric on her oversized overalls. Although they were only oversized because Ursula was as tiny as a wood sprite.

"Henry Rice!" she bellowed. (Tiny as a wood sprite but with the personality of a giant.) "Doctor Yates told you no more than one soda a day. That's your second this morning."

Henry defiantly dropped his head back and lifted the can straight up to drain it. He ended with a dramatic sigh. "I'm drinking ahead for tomorrow." He walked over and dropped the can in the recycling bin and headed out of the room.

31

I became Ursula's new focus. "Did I hear you say you weren't getting a tree? How can you celebrate without the smell of pine in the house?"

"I'm surrounded by the smell of pine every time I step outside, and my sisters have trees. Besides, my budget is tight because I'm paying several people a lot of money to renovate the inn." The last comment cut short her lecture.

She nodded. "You could wait until Christmas. The lot on Crimson Grove sells the leftover trees for seventy percent off that day."

"I'll think about it. In the meantime, I've got to get back to work." I tossed the dogs another treat and followed Ursula down the hallway.

"We're almost done with installing the crown moulding," Ursula said.

"That'll make someone happy," I muttered absently.

She looked back at me. "Oh? Who? Was Henry complaining about all the work to you?" she asked quickly, gearing up for another sibling argument.

"No, not at all. I was talking about Redford. The hammering makes him skittish. That's all." If my dogs only knew how often they became the scapegoat for my verbal blunders.

Ursula stopped at the end of the hallway. "Really? That's strange. Just this morning, he came into the dining room to hang out with us. Even fell asleep next to the tool box."

"Did he? I guess he's getting used to the noise then. I only know what my dog mom senses tell me. I'll see you later." I headed to the door before I tangled myself up any further.

CHAPTER 6

I parked near the newspaper office and headed on foot toward the hub of town where the festival was slowly growing in size and activity. Raine texted that she had booked three more card readings, the usual holiday rush, she noted, and that she'd have to skip our lunch date. I was just as glad. My detour home to see Mom and her holiday boyfriend surprise had thrown me off my schedule. I decided to grab a quick lunch and head toward the tent to interview the cast for the Dickens' play.

The two officers on mounted police duty seemed to be having a great time with their festival assignment. Normally, they didn't ride horses around town, only to parades and big events. A group of teenagers had stopped them for selfies with the horses, and they didn't seem to mind. It wasn't as if a holiday festival was a hot bed of crime. People were in cheery moods and too stuffed to the gills with festival goodies to cause trouble.

I headed past the selfie session and turned the corner to where the food kiosks had been set up. I knew there would be an over-load of food tonight at Emily's dinner, so I opted for a fresh roasted ear of corn. I'd save my mincemeat pie *adventure* for a lunch with Raine.

After applying copious amounts of parmesan butter on my well intentioned, once healthy corn on the cob, I was in the midst of a bite when a familiar voice rolled over my shoulder.

"Fancy meeting you here, Bluebird."

I hastily wiped butter from my mouth and swallowed before turning around. Detective Jackson was wearing a black windbreaker over his sweater and jeans. He'd pulled a black and red striped knit beanie down over long hair. It stuck out wildly as if he'd just snowboarded down a steep mountain. He lifted off his sunglasses and hung them on the front of his sweater. His amber eyes looked unearthly pale under the icy blue sky. That famous cocky grin of his lit up his face and nearly melted the parmesan butter right off my corn.

"There you are, Detective Jackson. I was beginning to think they moved you to an entirely new precinct." I rarely used his whole title but it had been a few weeks and we were in a very public setting so it seemed appropriate.

"No new precinct. We had several detectives and higher ups retire this year. They always leave just before the holidays. So I'm stuck doing double and triple duty." He motioned to the corn in my hand. "Is the corn good?"

"Hmm, not sure. I can't taste it underneath the slabs of parmesan butter. But I'm sure it's good and sweet and nutritious beneath all the fat."

"You've talked me into it." He approached the booth. Instantly, the two young girls taking orders had a tussle for space at the counter to help their newest customer. In the end, they compromised and one took the order while the other took the money. While he was busy ordering his corn, I took a few more bites of mine, certain that there was no way to make nibbling a greasy cob of corn look appealing or ladylike.

Jackson opted for a spicy chili powder mix over layers of butter. He took a bite and swallowed. "You're right. It's hard to tell there's corn underneath all the toppings."

"I really consider it more the serving vessel for the butter and cheese."

We decided to walk through the festivities with our mobile lunches. We caught plenty of stares and curious glances as we strolled through. Jackson was always seemingly oblivious to the amount of attention he attracted. I, on the other hand, was acutely aware of it.

"Working on anything exciting for the paper?" he asked.

"Yes, well, the *Junction Times* will be covering the arms deal in the Middle East and the terrible flu epidemic in Asia."

He glanced over at me with a skeptical brow.

"Yes, I'm kidding. Those are the topics I see when I'm deep asleep and having journalistic dreams. This week, I'm covering the local production of *A Christmas Carol.*"

He shook his head. "What a waste of your talent."

"Thank you. What about you? If you're covering for a lot of other people, you must be brow high in interesting cases. Anything you might need assistance with? I happen to know a nosy reporter and amateur sleuth that would love to be pulled from her current assignment."

"You'd be way more helpful than some of the rookies I'm working with, Bluebird. But I'm afraid you'll have to hang out with Ebenezer Scrooge this week."

"That's depressing. But I suppose it's for the best. My mom is in town for the holidays."

"Really? Mom Taylor is here. Cool."

"Yeah, cool," I repeated with far less enthusiasm.

We stopped at a cart selling hot cider. Jackson bought us each a cup. I dropped my mostly chiseled ear of corn into the trash can and took hold of the cider. I took a sip. The warm, comforting aroma of clove and cinnamon curled through the steam evaporating off the cup.

I blew on the drink for it too cool. It would be tragic to burn my taste buds before sitting down to one of Emily's delicious dinners.

"What's wrong with the mom visit? Too much unwanted advice? I know that half the time I spend with my mom, she's doling out advice on every aspect of my life." He took a sip of cider. "Even what kind of toothpaste I should be using."

"Yes, there's never any shortage of mom advice when she's around, but that's not it. She showed up with—get this—a new boyfriend."

"Cool," he said again.

"Is that going to be your default response for this conversation because, as you can tell, I'm not finding it all that cool." I sipped some cider. It was tangy and spicy.

"Why are you upset? Don't you want her to be happy?"

I looked up at him. He instantly read my expression. He was just a little too good at knowing what I was thinking. I brushed it off as a skill learned from being a detective and not from him knowing me too well already.

"You're mad because you think this guy is trying to replace your dad."

"Hello, Detective Jackson," two women said in sing-song voices as they strolled past in their Victorian dresses and bonnets.

"Ladies," he bowed his head and returned to our conversation. "Did I nail it?" he asked cockily.

"Fine. Yes. You nailed it. But don't let it go to your head. What's worse is I feel so childish about it all." For the first time since I'd learned about the boyfriend my throat tightened and I was blinking back tears. Jackson noticed. Naturally.

"Bluebird," he said quietly and in a tone that melted my heart a bit. It also made a tear break free. I wiped it quickly away.

"I was really close with my dad. My brother and my two sisters weren't into sports like me. Dad took me to all the practices. He came to every one of my softball and soccer games. Afterward, he'd take me out for pizza and he'd go over all the things I did right and wrong. We spent a lot of time together. I even helped him with his plumbing business every summer."

"Sunni, that's why he's irreplaceable. Your mom having a new friend has nothing to do with replacing your dad. It's just helping her live the rest of her life."

I stared up at him. "Why do you have to sound so reasonable? It makes me feel even more silly about this minor selfish breakdown."

He turned and dropped his arm around my shoulder. "Minor breakdowns are no big deal. Everyone needs one now and then." His phone beeped and he glanced at it. "I've got to head back to the station. Are you interested in going to the play tomorrow night?"

"You mean us? Together?"

"No, I thought we could each bring dates and meet up. Yes, you and me, together. Preferably sitting next to each other if that's all right."

I knuckled him lightly on the side. It was rock hard, of course. "I'd like that. My family will probably be around too, so be warned you may have to meet my mom."

"Looking forward to it. Where are you off to now?"

"Like you," I said. "Back to work. I've got a date with Ebenezer Scrooge."

"I'll pick you up at your place tomorrow at six," he said as he walked away.

It seemed my day was looking up.

CHAPTER 7

There was just enough constructive chaos under the theater tent to make me stay out of the way and observe. Sometimes I gathered more information just by watching from the sidelines. Scottie had pointed out a few of the key players and mentioned they'd have time for interviews shortly before she hurried off to take care of a technical problem with the sound system.

I sat on one of the folding chairs set up for tomorrow night's performance. I pulled out my notebook, planning to write out some questions, but found my thoughts drifting right along toward Jackson. It would be our first proper public outing together. In fact, most of the town would be sitting under the same tent. There were sure to be scrutinizing looks and secret gossipy texts, but I could handle it. Hopefully.

"What on earth took you so long, Tim?" The snippy forty-something man had a sharp, arrogant chin with a deep cleft. His auburn hair was parted to the side and combed with some kind of gel product. He looked a little too clean shaven and not quite grizzled enough to play the part of Scrooge, but Scottie had pointed him out as the leading man, Evan Weezer.

The tall, thin thirty-something man he'd called Tim had a thin mouth that disappeared completely as Mr. Weezer berated him for taking so long to deliver a bottle of water.

Weezer held out his hand. "Where's my change?"

Tim dug into the pocket of his coat and fished out what appeared to be a quarter. He placed it on Weezer's palm. With the way he inspected the coin before sticking it into his own pocket, I half expected Weezer to bite down on it to make sure it was real. It seemed the man might have been appropriately cast into the role of Scrooge. The similarities between the actor and infamous character continued when Tim, an apparent employee of Weezer's, hesitantly asked for a favor.

"Mr. Weezer," Tim said rubbing his hands together, only not from the cold weather. "Tim Junior is playing his first game today on the traveling soccer team. I promised him I'd be there to watch. If I could leave the office two hours early today—"

"Two hours!" Weezer barked as if the man had asked him for a month long vacation. "You haven't finished the flyers for the open house, and I need you to make some cold calls to prospective clients. Two hours is out of the question. You can leave twenty minutes early, and I consider that to be generous." Weezer straightened his collar with an imperious chin lift.

Tim's face grew stiff. I couldn't tell if it was anger or more fear. "But I'll miss the game."

"It's a silly soccer game. How will you pay for Timmy's soccer uniform if you're out of a job?" With that, he turned sharply on his heels to let Tim know the conversation had ended. Weezer's skewering gaze landed on me. I glanced quickly away pretending to be interested in the set decorations on stage.

"You're the reporter," Weezer said with some degree of civility.

"I'm ready for my interview. But I don't have much time. I'm the lead actor."

It took me a second to gather myself. I got up from the chair. "Fine, yes, that's great. Should we talk here or do you prefer somewhere else?"

"I have my own trailer behind the tent, of course," he added. Apparently, the man considered himself to be a mega movie star. "But to save time, we can just talk here."

I put out my hand. "Sunni Taylor from the *Junction Times*. Thank you for taking the time to talk with me."

As he shook my hand, he used his free hand to pull out a stack of fancy gold leaf business cards. "Here you go. And extras to give family and friends. I'm the top selling agent in the state, and I'd be happy to list your home. Are you interested in selling?" No wonder he was the top seller. He'd managed to flip the interview right into a realty sales pitch before I got out one question.

"I'm not looking to sell anytime soon." I thought about the inn in all its unfinished, crumbling glory as the subject of an open house flyer. It made me smile. I placed the cards in my pocket. "Thank you, though. If I know someone looking to sell, I now have a recommendation." I patted my pocket.

He rubbed his clean shaven chin. A cleft was normally appealing in a chin, but his made him look mean. It might have been because his chin was exceptionally pointed. Or perhaps it was my early assessment of his character after watching him with Tim.

"Sunni Taylor?" he said as a question. "Are you the woman who is trying to bring back that old wreck, the Cider Ridge Inn?" His snide tone and words left no room for misinterpretation. He thought the renovation was a waste of time but then he would. He only saw dollar signs when he looked at properties.

"Why yes," I said with forced politeness. "I am *that* Sunni Taylor."

He clucked his tongue loudly. "Such a shame. That stretch of land where the inn and those old farmhouses sit are a developers' dream purchase."

I was alarmed at how quickly I could wholly and utterly dislike someone. How did such an arrogant man make so many real estate deals? No doubt his ruthless character had more to do with his success than being a good salesperson.

"Those old farmhouses belong to my sisters. The property belonged to my mother's family. Maybe that's a good thing. I can't think of anything more horrible than having that picturesque piece of land crowded with cookie cutter tract homes."

His mouth tightened. It seemed Mr. Weezer wasn't used to being contradicted. I worried briefly that I'd just lost a key inter-view for my article. If I had, it was worth it.

"Anyhow," he huffed, "ask your questions, then I'll tell you the information I want listed in the article."

I stared down at my notebook. He had information for the arti-cle. Could it be that the information would be all about his busi-ness and nothing about the play, I thought wryly. Well, Parker warned me that it was basically free advertising space for future marketing opportunities.

"Let's get started then. I want to make sure I've spelled your name correctly."

"It's on my card. Evan with an A and two Es in Weezer. Evan Weezer," he said succinctly.

"Right, Evan Weezer," I said as I wrote it. A laugh spurted from my mouth. I smiled up at him. "You're Evan Weezer and you're playing the part of Ebenezer." I chuckled again. He didn't seem to catch the irony. It seemed he wasn't a fan of humor.

"Yes, that's right," he said sternly.

I cleared my throat. "Right, well then. Is theater acting a hobby of yours? How much experience do you have on stage?"

"I run a very busy realty company. I hardly have time for a

hobby. I did occasionally play parts in high school. In fact, the drama teacher said I was a natural."

I wrote down his comment, which helped me hide the smile that was working to break free. I collected myself and peered up at him. "Are you a fan of Dickens?"

His face contorted for a second. "Why would I be a fan of Dickens Realty? They do shoddy contract work. They consider themselves to be one of my fiercest competitors, but I assure you, they aren't."

"Actually," I said quietly. "I meant Charles Dickens. The author of the original *A Christmas Carol*."

"Of course I know who Charles Dickens is." He'd turned it around to make me feel like the foolish person even though he was clearly in the silly seat for his response.

He pulled out his phone, checked it and quickly dashed off a text. "I'm short on time. Please make note of this." He waved imperiously at my notebook. "Weezer Realty is number one in the county and the state. On average, we sell houses in less than two weeks time and at asking price. I have been voted top real estate agent three times in a row. Then use my card to make sure my contact information is prominent in the article."

I nodded. "I'll do that. Thank you for your time, Mr. Weezer." He walked off in a self-important manner.

CHAPTER 8

*W*hile I waited for my next interview, the rhythmic clip-clop of horse hooves pulled my attention to the street outside the tent. A shiny black open carriage rolled past behind two coffee brown horses. The horses' bridles were decorated with holly and red bows and the carriage offered riders lush velvet seating. I immediately recognized the driver of the carriage as Aurora, the woman who had sparked the morning's Disney princess debate.

"Did Evan Weezer Scrooge fill your head with all his delusions of grandeur?" the deep voice said from behind.

I turned to face a fifty-something man who was well over six feet tall and carried a great deal of weight around his middle. He hadn't spoken loudly, but his deep voice nearly billowed out the canvas walls of the tent. His giant hand shot forward and swallowed mine completely.

"Danny Danforth, a.k.a. Ghost of Christmas Present." He pointed out his sweater and slacks. "I promise my costume will be more elaborate than this. This is my realty disguise."

"Sunni Taylor of the *Junction Times*. So, you're an agent too?"

He reached for his pocket. "Oops, I forgot my business cards in the car. Danforth Realty, formerly known as Danforth Realty, number one in the state."

He looked back toward where people were rehearsing lines on stage. Scottie was directing, all while handing out orders to the set crew. No one could do multitasking like a teacher, and Scottie was doing her profession proud this afternoon. Evan Weezer was nowhere in sight.

Danny turned back to me. I was already getting a crick in my neck from having to stare up at him.

"I suppose Weezer told you he was number one in the state." He laughed. "Of course he did. He'd have it tattooed on his forehead if he could. Well, don't let his bragging fool you. He didn't get there by any ethical means. Scammed and skimmed and stole my clients all the way to the top." Danny waved his large hand. "But that's not why you're here. What would you like to know and before you bother to ask, I'm six-foot-five and my feet are a size fifteen."

I dropped my gaze down to his shiny black loafers. They were big enough to sail a small family around a lake. "Wow, yes, they are big." I lifted my face up to him. "I suppose you need them to stay upright in the wind."

His thunderous laugh startled everyone in the tent, including me and I'd seen it coming. Just as the echo of his laughter subsided, screams filled the tent as a corner of the large structure broke free and fluttered wildly in the breeze. With one corner waving like a sail in a storm, the rest of the tent creaked and folded. The walls began to collapse around us. Danny and I both ran for the open corner. Frantic chaos followed. People inside and outside of the tent worked together to capture and control the loose corner.

Danny took command of the situation. "The corner stake is missing," he bellowed as his large fingers gripped the canvas. I stood between Evan's assistant Tim and the woman with puffy eyes I'd seen earlier setting up the Nativity manger. With six of us holding the canvas captive, we managed to keep the tent from collapsing in on itself as someone found an extra stake to pound into the corner. Danny and two other members of the crew got the rogue corner secured. A round of applause followed for those of us who'd kept a full on calamity from taking place. We added in our own round of high-fives for flawless teamwork before dispersing.

Evan came out from a white trailer looking baffled by the commotion. "What's going on?" he asked.

Danny blew a raspberry from his lips. "Never you mind, Weezer. Go back to your prince's trailer and take a beauty nap or something. The rest of us have it under control."

A flush of angry red appeared from beneath Evan's collar and spread over his face. "If you're in control, then we're all in trouble, you worthless—"

Scottie's sharp clap stopped him from finishing his insult. "Now that the excitement is over, we need to start our rehearsal. I need the tent cleared of anyone who is not involved with the play. No previews or early peeks." Scottie smiled at me. "I'm sorry but that includes reporters. I'm sure there'll be time for some interviews early tomorrow."

"No problem." I only had a little information, but something told me it wouldn't matter too much. I just needed to list all the important contact information for the cast members' businesses and the article would be considered a success. "I'll see you tomorrow." I headed back through the tent.

"Thanks for your help," Danny's baritone voice rumbled behind me.

I turned back and waved. "Glad I could help."

I headed through the front tent flaps just before they were sealed shut for rehearsal. The street had grown even more crowded. The festival was starting to really take off. I wasn't paying attention as I hopped off the sidewalk to cross to the other side and just missed a warm steamy pile of horse manure.

I laughed to myself. "Nothing more Victorian than that."

CHAPTER 9

*W*hile Lana had gone for the elegant, rustic look in her holiday decor, Emily had opted for charming country. Wreaths of dried orange slices tied up with rafia and bundles of cinnamon sticks dangled across the reclaimed wood mantel on the stone fireplace. My little sister had decorated an old, weathered wagon wheel with greenery and tiny pine cones. The bottom was finished off with a massive red and green plaid bow. The wheel, with all its festoonery, hung proudly over the hearth where Christmas stockings made from printed feed bags hung from brass hooks. Her tree was an adorable mix of linen bows, teensy sparkling stars and decorated gingerbread men. Redford and Newman trotted right over to the tree that seemed to miraculously be growing cookies from its limbs.

"No way you two. Sit down over there. I don't want to be blamed for headless gingerbread ornaments," I scolded.

"I stupidly allowed the goats to walk through the room this morning." Emily took the bottle of wine I'd brought, my usual contribution to family dinners. "I lost three ornaments before I realized what a mistake it had been."

"Ah, my girls, I miss them. Do I have time to visit Tinkerbell and Cuddlebug before dinner?" I'd become an aunt to the cutest pair of goats on the planet, and I couldn't get enough of the little darlings.

Emily took hold of my arm. "No, you're not getting out of social time. Everyone's in the kitchen filling Christmas Crackers for the festival. Lana's idea, of course. She said it's not a Victorian Christmas without them. Although I doubt they added in slivers of paper advertising a party business back in the nineteenth century."

I shook my head. "That woman never stops being a business barracuda."

Emily tilted her head. "I don't know if Lana can be categorized as a barracuda." She moved her chin side to side. "Actually, it fits." She stopped me before reaching the kitchen. "What do you think of Mom's new friend?" she whispered. "Nick is giving him a tour of the farm right now. They had to carry flashlights," she said with an eye roll. "But you know how proud Nick is of his farm."

"As he should be. It's perfect. Love your decorations too, by the way. I'm glad I can come here and to Lana's for holiday cheer. I seem to be lacking it this year. Which brings me to your prior question. Why didn't Mom warn us ahead of time?" I nodded at her. "Yes, that sounded just like sixteen-year-old Sunni. I apologize but my teenage self has been rearing her silly head all day today."

"I think Mom kept it a surprise because she worried it might ruffle some feathers, especially with a certain daughter." She looked pointedly at me.

"If she'd told me ahead of time, it would have given me some time to prepare mentally. He seems like a very nice man though. I'm sure my teenage self will slowly fade back into history . . . eventually."

We walked into the kitchen. The warm aromas circling the room made my stomach rumble. I pressed my arm against my belly to quiet it.

Mom held up a shiny gold tubular package tied on each end with a white ribbon. "I think I'm getting the hang of these." She shook it once. "I hope I remembered to put in each of the treats."

"As long as you didn't forget the important one." Lana held up the thin blue strip of paper with her party planning advertisement."

"Thank goodness the Taylor family hasn't succumbed to the commercialization of Christmas," Emily quipped.

I had a good laugh as I pulled up a chair next to Mom. Lana passed over a shiny rectangle of paper and an empty toilet paper tube. "The long, thin piece of cardboard is the cracker snap. It goes through the middle of the tube and sticks out on each end."

"That's how two people crack it apart," Mom added. She pulled a few bowls of wrapped candies and plastic snowflakes closer. "Fill the tube with the goodies, and don't forget Lana's advertisement." Mom leaned closer. "I forgot one and had to redo the whole thing." The smell of her perfume, the same kind she'd been wearing since I was old enough to realize that the floral scent wasn't just part of Mom's own natural sweetness, sent a spark of longing for my childhood through me. I couldn't stop myself from giving her a kiss on the cheek.

"I'm glad you're here, Mom."

She wrapped her arm around my shoulder for a squeeze. "Where else would I rather be than with my beautiful daughters. I just wish Neal had found the time to visit. Last I heard he was in Thailand or something like that." She shook her head forlornly. "It's so hard having him traipse around the world, but I suppose he's happy. And it's important to be happy." She flicked her eyes my direction to let me know her last comment was meant mostly toward me. Mom reached over and squeezed my hand. "How did work go today?"

"Not terrific. I have to interview some of the cast members about the play. They're all local business people. My first interview was with the man playing Scrooge, and boy, did he fit the part. He's sharp, abrupt and kind of mean. And get this—his name is Evan Weezer. Quite the phonetic irony."

Emily and Mom laughed.

Lana picked up one of her advertisements. "Oh, that man is so pushy. Never stops shoving his business card into people's faces." With that, she shoved the tiny strip of paper with her contact information between the hard candies and plastic snowflakes.

"Not the only form of irony around the table tonight," Emily quipped and exchanged a secret wink with me.

The back door to the kitchen opened. Nick and Chris stomped their shoes on the doormat before walking into the kitchen. "Hmm, Emi, those scalloped potatoes smell so good." Nick patted his stomach. "I'm hungry enough to eat the entire dish on my own."

Mom immediately straightened her posture when Chris stepped into view. "What did you think of the farm?" Mom asked.

"Like it came right out of a country painting," Chris said. He was wearing a pale green sweater that had a picture of Rudolph embroidered into the fabric. "But I have to say my favorite part of the tour was the goats."

I perked up at the mention of my *girls*.

"They are quite the cutest thing I've ever seen," Chris continued.

One solid point gained in the liking Chris column. Anyone who saw the mind-boggling adorableness of Tinkerbell and Cuddlebug could not be all bad.

"I'll have to visit them tomorrow during the day," Mom said. "I can't picture myself hiking around the farm in the dark. Too many ways to break a hip."

Lana, Emily and I had a good laugh at her comment.

Mom looked somewhat hurt by our response. "Why is the vision of your mom breaking a hip so funny?"

"Glass of wine in the living room, Chris?" Nick asked, with a head motion letting him know it was a good time to duck out. The men scurried away with two glasses and the wine.

I plucked up some candies for the cracker. "It's not funny, of course, Mom. But how old do you think you are?"

"Old enough to break a hip," Mom replied sharply.

Lana placed another finished cracker on the growing pile. She was like an automated machine when it came to creating party goods. "Anyone is old enough to break a hip, Mom. It's just we consider hip breaking a plight of the very old, like eighty or ninety."

Mom shuffled in her seat, showing her agitation. My sisters and I exchanged guilty looks. We'd obviously hit a nerve with mom.

"You girls just wait until you reach your sixties. You'll see what I mean. I can feel my bones turning to powder as I sit here. But that might be because I'm slowly starving to death while being forced to stuff and wrap toilet paper tubes."

Emily got up and gave Mom a hug. "I'll start getting the plates ready. We're sorry, Mom. It's just none of us want to believe that you're getting older. You have to stay Mom forever."

Mom's soft, pink cheeks plumped back up with a smile. "Well, as much as I'd like to stay around forever, I haven't figured out how to do that. That's why I hope you girls will understand why I've started this new friendship with Chris."

All eyes were suddenly on me.

"I'm accepting it," I said hesitantly. "Slowly but surely. I want you to be happy, Mom. That's all that matters. And since Chris seems to understand the magic of Tinkerbell and Cuddlebug, I think he'll grow on me quickly."

"That's wonderful to hear, Sunni." Mom turned to Emily. "Now when do we eat? Your poor Mom is wasting away, powder bones and all."

CHAPTER 10

*A*fter a slightly tumultuous start to the evening, Emily's dinner party ended with all of us nearly comatose from good food and laughter. Chris had a marvelous wit, and it had been years since I'd seen my mom laugh so much.

I'd had two helpings of Emily's rich and decadent potatoes au gratin and two pieces of her caramel brown butter cake. My entire body had been moving slowly all morning in a sort of food hangover, but a brisk walk to town in the wintry chill blowing down from the mountains pepped me right up.

Scottie Sherman texted that the cast had arrived for the dress rehearsal and since she'd shooed me off so abruptly the day before, she was going to make it up to me by letting me hang around before dress rehearsal. But I was under strict orders not to take pictures. She didn't want the costumes and makeup to be seen before the performance.

Two teenage boys were standing guard when I reached the tent entrance. One boy, who was taking his security role quite seriously, stepped in front of me. "No one is allowed inside the tent while cast members rehearse." His voice was just changing, and it cracked halfway through his speech. But that didn't shake his confidence.

"Actually"—I pulled out my press identification—"I'm with the *Junction Times* and Mrs. Sherman is expecting me."

"Yeah, that's right, Tucker," the other boy said. "Remember when Mrs. Sherman told us we could let in the reporter?"

Tucker hesitated and stared down at me, trying to assess whether I was legit or up to no good. He seemed to land on legit. He stepped back, glanced furtively around to make sure no one passing by caught a glimpse of the activity within and opened the tent flap just enough for me to squeeze inside.

Chaos was in full motion under the big top. The first set was the scene from inside Scrooge's shop. A giant multi-paned window revealed the snowy village outside. The dark gloomy shop interior was lit only by two candle nubs and the fire in the hearth fizzled with just a tiny red flame. The set decorations were nice but the costumes and makeup were nothing short of Broadway caliber.

Scottie came scuttling out of the huddle of people with a light green program in her hand. She passed it to me. "These finally came back from the printers. They'll tell you the names of each character, and their business information is printed right below their names. It should help with your article."

I looked down at the program. A picture of an English village was printed across the cover. Beneath it were the words, "You're Invited to Charles Dickens' *A Christmas Carol*".

"Thank you, Scottie. This will help me keep names straight. By the way, the costumes and makeup are amazing."

"Aren't they?" She gazed around the room wearing a grin from ear to ear. The man playing Scrooge's dead partner, Jacob Marley, shuffled past wrapped in cumbersome plastic chains. His face was covered with pale yellow foundation and dark rings were smudged under his eyes. His entire head and chin were wrapped in the macabre, traditional bandage Victorian undertakers used to keep corpses from going slack-jawed in preparation for burial. It was hard to tell whether the actor, Hubert Cummings, owner of a local funeral home, coincidentally enough, was having a harder time with the chains or the bandage on his head. Either way, he looked properly creepy, just as a haunting spirit should, I thought and then quickly breathed a sigh of relief that my own spirit looked far more dashing than dead.

"Just wonderful, Scottie. You've done such a great job." I decided it couldn't hurt to heap on the praise. She'd been more than generous by allowing me in on the top secret dress rehearsal.

"I'm so glad you think so." Then she pointed a teacher finger at me. "Now remember—no pictures. We don't want anyone to see the cast until tonight's performance."

"I promise. No pictures." Her admonition reminded me about my theater date with Jackson. I was a mix of excitement and nerves about the evening. "Of course I'll be at the performance tonight. Looking forward to it."

"Marvelous," she chirped. A clamor and loud voices on stage grabbed her attention. "I better get up there before someone throws a fist. Opening day jitters have everyone on edge." She hurried off.

"So, the reporter has returned to the scene of the crime," a baritone voice said from behind. I turned around and came face to face with an impressive Ghost of Christmas Present. Danny Danforth wore a dark green satin coat that hung to the floor, or at least tried to with his impossible height. The collar, bell shaped sleeves and hem of the coat were trimmed in fake gray fur. A thick fuzzy brown beard, a few shades darker than his hair, had been glued to his face and his naturally thick brows had been enhanced too. His big head was crowned with a wreath of holly leaves.

Danny held out his arms. He had an enormous *wingspan*. "What do you think? Christmas ghost from my head"—he peered up to get a glimpse of the wreath on his head—"to almost my toes." He looked down at his shoes. They were the same black loafers from the day before. "There wasn't enough time to find shoes my size to fit the costume. Although, who really knows what type of shoes a spirit should be wearing. Frankly, if I'm ever a ghost, I hope I'm barefoot."

His comment made me smile. Poor Edward had been stuck for eternity in stiff, new Hessian boots. I hoped things were better for him this morning, now that Ursula and Henry had moved on to patching walls, a much quieter task.

"I must say you really fit the part," I said. "You're just what I would expect the Ghost of Christmas Present to look like." I pulled out my notebook. "Scottie gave me the program so I have your contact information, which I'll be sure to include in the article. How are you feeling about this year's play? Are you looking forward to the performance?"

"Hmm," Danny said and made a show of pretending to rub his beard in thought. "I can see why guys like these big beards. Makes me feel important and serious." This agent was certainly more delightful to talk to than the number one real estate agent.

He cleared his throat. "I'm proud of what we've accomplished here. Scottie has done a great job. I think people will be pleased. You can quote me on all that. Now for my off the record comment. I wish that Weezer hadn't been cast in the lead. He already thinks he's far superior to the rest of us. But then, he *does* mirror his character in many ways." Danny laughed at his own comment. The thunderous sound reminded me of the day before when a wind gust sent the corner of the tent sailing up like a runaway kite.

"By the way, did they ever find out what happened to the tent yesterday? Did the missing tent stake show up?"

He shook his head. "I don't think so but I left early to meet with a potential client."

"Danny," Scottie called from the stage. "Danny, we need you."

"Time for my lines already?" he asked. "I haven't even seen Marley on stage yet."

Scottie held up a brass lantern. "No, we need you to hang the lanterns on the street poles."

"Of course, always call the tall guy instead of dragging out the ladder. Nice talking to you again, Miss Taylor. But I'm off. Giant duty calls."

"Thank you."

I hadn't seen Ebenezer Scrooge walking down from the side exit of the stage until Danny's large physique moved out of view. The two men skewered one another with scowls as they walked past each other. Evan had a black top hat on a gray wig and mutton chops glued to the sides of his face. He was wearing a black frock coat over a gray vest. The makeup team had added dark scowl lines to his forehead and face. They looked perfectly at home on his pinched face.

"Those two can produce a winter storm with the way they look at each other." The woman stuck out her hand. "I'm Carly Gomez." She held out her arms displaying long flowing sleeves made from lacy white gauze. "Ghost of Christmas Past, in case the pale white makeup and long dress didn't give it away." She stared down at the dress with its frilly collar and adornments. "It's sort of a gothic mix of a bridal gown and a nightgown. At least I'm not wearing a tattered old hooded cloak like Brian, the music shop owner. He's playing the Ghost of Christmas Yet to Be."

I smiled admiringly at her. "Your costume does sort of look like something a vampire might wear to bed, but it's lovely and very ghost-like. I'm Sunni Taylor," I added.

"Yes, the reporter from the *Junction Times*. I own Fuzz, Fur and Fins Pet Shop in Hickory Flats."

"I thought I recognized you. Not with the pasty white complexion, of course. I buy my dogs' favorite bacon treats at your store. They love them."

"Yes, the bacon flavored treats are a customer favorite. I was hoping to get a quick word with you before the rehearsal starts. I see Scottie gave you the program. It has all my relevant contact information, but I was hoping you could add a bit in about our annual pet adoption day. It's on December 29th in our parking lot."

I opened my notebook. "I will make sure to mention it. It sounds like a good cause."

"We generally end up matching every dog and cat with a new owner. What kind of dogs do you have?"

Before I could answer, several shrieks and a general clamor came from the stage side of the tent. The large painted backdrops were falling down a like a strand of dominoes. People rushed forward to stop them from ripping and bending, but the heart-breaking sound of cardboard shredding filled the air. It was followed by a gasp. Scrooge's shop window had been ripped in half, effectively splitting the window down the middle.

"Oh wow, that's going to set us back. I better go see what I can do to help." Carly headed off.

"I'll be sure to feature the adoption day in the article."

I watched for a few minutes as everyone, with the exception of Evan, scrambled to make sure there was no more damage to the set. Evan was standing away from the noise, talking on the phone. As he spoke, his assistant Tim, came out from behind the stage. His face was pale with worry as he searched anxiously around for his boss. He spotted Evan and took a deep, steadying breath before walking toward him. His fingers anxiously tugged at the bottom of his coat as he neared Evan.

Evan looked up from his conversation but then turned and kept pacing. Anyone, and most especially someone who knew Tim, could see that he was distraught about something. He finally got the courage to follow behind Evan. He reached up with a shaky hand and tapped Evan on the shoulder.

Evan spun around with a deep, angry scowl, a perfectly

Scrooge expression, but Tim held his ground and straightened his posture to speak. "I need to leave. My son hurt his ankle in soccer practice."

Evan said something quickly into his phone and hung up. "But we're not finished at the office yet, and I need you to answer calls and questions while I'm on stage."

Tim shrank down some under Evan's glower, which was made that much scarier by the makeup and fake mutton chops. "Helen says it might be broken, and Timmy is asking for his dad."

I pretended to be reading something on my phone, but my ear was trained on the conversation. It was hard to believe anyone was as awful as Evan Weezer. He huffed and puffed and muttered something under his breath.

"You'll have to work late tomorrow to make up for it," Evan growled.

Tim nodded appreciatively, although his boss hardly deserved any kind of thanks. "I'll work late tomorrow, but I really must be off right now. Timmy is waiting for me."

Evan waved him away as if he couldn't stand the sight of him. Tim hurried away on long thin legs, his shoulders a little more erect and more color in his face. It made me wonder if Evan had said no would Tim just have accepted the decision? It certainly didn't seem like a job worth saving. There had to be better people to work for than Evan Weezer Scrooge.

Aside from the damaged set panel, the stage was ready for the rehearsal to start. Scottie came down the steps to stand in front of the stage. She was holding a mega phone. "Let's take places for scene one," she bellowed into the speaker.

I walked up next to her. "I'll be on my way. I don't want to spoil the play for tonight. Thanks for letting me hang out."

"I'm sorry about the chaos. We'll have to repair and paint that set. We're out of cardboard." She bit her lip in distress.

"Is there something wrong?" I asked.

She sighed and it was accidentally broadcast through the mega phone. She switched it off. "No, nothing's wrong. I'm just being silly and superstitious, but after the tent fiasco and now the set collapse, I can't help worrying that they were bad omens and that this play is headed for disaster."

"Nonsense. I'm sure that's just opening day jitters. The stage and actors look terrific. It'll be fine. I'll see you later. And break a leg," I said as I walked away.

"That's only for the cast members," she said in a fretful voice.

I stopped. "Sorry. Then scratch that. Good wishes for a big success." I hurried out of the tent with cheeks flaming pink about my misstep.

My phone buzzed in my pocket as I stepped into the fresh air. The *guards* were still standing out front, only they'd grown bored and had shirked their duty to have a snowball fight.

I ducked out of the way of a flying sphere of snow and pulled out my phone. It was a text from Raine.

"How about getting that mincemeat pie?"

"Absolutely yes. I need the break."

CHAPTER 11

"The best part of this pie is the flaky crust," I said as I folded the last half of my mincemeat pie into a napkin.

"Is that all you're eating?" Raine asked.

"Yes, as predicted, fruit and meat mixed together is not really my thing. Besides, Emily baked a feast last night, and I have little control when it comes to Emily's cooking. And I've got a da—" I paused and peered over at Raine.

Her eyes were round and sparkly. "Yes, go on. You were saying something about a date?" she prodded.

"No, I was going to say *day*, I've got—a day of stuff to do." I waved my arm around. "Journalistic stuff for the day."

She lifted her nose. "Fine, don't tell your best friend about your date." She pulled her knitted shawl higher on her shoulders.

"All right. I'm going to the play tonight with a *friend*. It might be a date. I'm not sure. It seems like it."

Raine stopped and turned to me in the middle of a rather bustling sidewalk. She crossed her arms. "Detective Brady Jackson asked you to the play and you didn't tell me?"

"And this is why. You're treating the causal, impromptu outing as if he'd gotten down on a knee and proposed to me. It's no big deal."

Raine's eyes rounded again as her attention was pulled away by something behind me.

"He's walking this way, isn't he?" I asked.

"Yup. And, might I add, he looks spectacular in a gunmetal gray sweater."

I reached up to wipe my mouth. "Do I have any food on my face?" I asked quickly.

"Too late to do anything about it now," Raine said and flashed a brilliant, white smile. "Detective Jackson," she said with a little tune, "I see you're out and about, keeping the festival safe and trouble free."

I wiped my mouth once more and turned to look at him. His amber gaze drew me in like a magnet. Then he pulled it away to respond to Raine. "Actually, just like everyone else, I'm out here to eat."

"You should try the mincemeat pie," Raine suggested. "They're delicious."

Jackson's lip turned up slightly. "Not sure if the meat and fruit combo works for me."

Raine secretly jabbed me as if that coincidence meant we were destined to be together forever.

As Raine continued her conversation with Jackson, my eyes drifted around to find the source of a familiar laugh. It was my Mom's laugh, the flirty one. I froze with terror. It seemed the entire family was going to meet Detective Jackson in one impromptu sidewalk chat.

Everyone's curious gazes fell immediately on the tall, dashing detective standing next to me. "Looks like you're about to meet the entire Taylor trio," I muttered from the side of my mouth.

"I thought that might be your mom. You look like her," he muttered back.

"Fancy meeting all of you here," Lana said cheerily. She dropped right into gracious introduction mode. Her hand went out. "I know we've met before, less formally. I'm Lana, Sunni's sister." I noticed she left off the adjective *older* in her greeting. Before I could utter even a single word, Lana burst right into the other introductions. "This is Maggie, our mom and our youngest sister, Emily." This time she used the qualifier.

"Brady Jackson. Nice to meet all of you," Jackson said. "I was just telling Sunni how much she looked like her mother."

That comment earned a girlish giggle from my mom. It was a new laugh that I'd never heard before. (Apparently one she saved for extraordinarily handsome detectives.) I half expected her to coyly pull at a strand of hair as she smiled up at him. "That's so nice to hear. Sunni and I have a lot of similarities."

I tried to figure out what those similarities were other than the shape of our eyes and skin tone, but my attention was instantly diverted when Jackson turned to Emily to ask her a question. I immediately felt the twinge of envy I always felt when a man turned his attention to my beautiful blonde sister. It was a stupid reaction, but I couldn't stop it.

"You sell organic eggs out at your farm, right?" he asked. "What hours are you open? I've been meaning to buy some."

"Great," Emily said. Unlike my mom, she hadn't added any giggle or flirty blink to her response. She didn't need to. "I think I have a business card. It has the hours listed on the back." Emily dug through her purse for the card. Mom used the lull in conversation to jump into Mom mode.

"So, Detective Jackson, how do you two know each other? My daughter hasn't been in some kind of trouble with the law, has she?" She chuckled at the end of the absurd question.

"Yes, Mom. We met when he foiled my armed bank robbery."

"She was quite the wily little culprit," Jackson continued. "Actually, Sunni's helped out on a few murder cases. Her investigative skills are impressive."

Lana knew darn well I'd been working on murder cases, but she put on a show of shock and surprise. "Wow, Sunni, that's amazing."

Emily and I exchanged brief eye rolls.

"Well, dear, don't do anything dangerous. You let the detective handle the scary stuff," Mom said.

"Darn." I peered up at Jackson, who was holding back a grin. "I guess that means no more sending me in first when we're about to take down the bad guy."

Mom made a tsk-tsk sound. "I guess I've been properly chastised for being a worry wart. Just wait until you have children of your own." She looked pointedly between Jackson and me. I wondered if a hole could just open up in the icy sidewalk and suck me away.

"Let's get some lunch," Emily said abruptly as she handed him her card. She winked at me and moved to whisk her two lunch mates away.

Mom leaned in to whisper something to me on her way past. "And they'd be beautiful grandchildren at that."

We waited for them to be well on their way, waving again at Lana and Mom as they turned into a kiosk selling knitted hats and scarves.

"Well, that was unexpected," I chirped, not knowing what else to say.

Jackson absently put his hand against the back of my coat. "It was nice seeing them. I'll see you tonight."

"Yes. I'll be ready. It should be a good play. I got a special peek at the costumes and makeup at dress rehearsal. They were impressive."

"Sounds good. See you later, Raine. And don't conjure up too many spirits this season. I've got enough live troublemakers to keep me busy through next year."

Raine laughed. "Not making any promises on that front."

We watched him walk away.

"Lucky girl," Raine muttered.

"Not feeling that lucky." We pulled our coat collars up. The temperature was dropping and every word came out with a burst of white condensation. "I was hoping to prep my mom before meeting Jax for the first time. But at least that bandage has been yanked free. Hopefully, during the second meeting, she won't bring up something humiliating about my childhood, like how I always wore so much dirt I left a ring around the bathtub or some sweet little nugget like that."

Raine laughed as she linked her arm around mine. "I'm going to make sure I'm there for the second meeting. I think it will be well worth the wait."

CHAPTER 12

I leaned into the bathroom mirror to add another layer of mascara. Newman and Redford had plopped down in the hallway while I finished getting ready. The frigid air outside really narrowed down my wardrobe choices, which may or may not have been a good thing. It shortened my decision time but left me with few things that could be considered date attire. Or was I jumping ahead on calling it a date? Jackson had never used the word. Another bleak thought struck me. How many other women had he asked first? I laughed that notion off. After all, how many women would have said no when he asked?

I stepped back and blew a raspberry at my reflection. "Silly woman." The years tossed away on my first steady boyfriend had left me with little confidence when it came to dating. And wasn't it just like me to dive back into the whole thing with Brady Jackson. It was like learning how to train sharks and hopping right into the great white shark tank to get started.

I smoothed my hands down the forest green knit dress. I'd pulled on shiny black boots and even added a white cashmere scarf to top off the scooped collar of the dress. The look felt somewhat festive. I was still glancing at the mirror as I stepped out of the bathroom and tripped over Newman. My boots left a nice dent in the wooden floor as I hopped and stumbled a few steps before catching myself just as I entered the kitchen.

"Always a delight to see you moving gracefully about the house," Edward drawled from his perch over the kitchen hearth. He glanced down at my boots and then looked pointedly at his own feet. "Just making sure I'm still wearing mine. Yours look strikingly similar. Perhaps my fashion sense is wearing off on you. Although, those pointy heels would hardly be practical in a stirrup. No need for riding spurs, I suppose."

"Well, then it's lucky I'm not riding any horses tonight. And as to your fashion sense—" I looked at his blue waistcoat, breeches and tall boots. "Actually, I've got no snide comment. I love to see men dressed in nineteenth century garb. As long as I don't have to wear hoops and corsets."

I decided to fill the wait time with the mindless task of unloading the dishwasher. "These boots are just for show." I wiggled my toes and discovered there was little room. "I'm certain my feet will make me rethink my choice by the end of the night."

Edward floated over to the kitchen counter and peered down at me from his new perch. "What do you mean they're for show? Who are you *showing* them to?"

"If you must know—"

"Of course I must, why would I have asked you otherwise?"

I pulled several cups out of the rack. "No, that's just a phrase we use. Never mind. I'm going to a play with a friend. That's all. So when he gets here, you'll need to disappear."

He drifted down and stood directly next to the dishwasher, crossing his arms and ankles as he hovered just inches over the floor watching me like a great black crow. I continued my task unabated.

"Since you're avoiding eye contact, I can only assume this friend you speak of is the man with the wild hair and wolfish eyes."

"He doesn't have wild hair and wolfish eyes." A knife slipped from my fingers and clanged on the floor. I picked it up and dropped it back into the utensil rack for another wash.

"Yes, he does," Edward said emphatically. I'd learned it was never easy winning any kind of debate with a stubborn, arrogant ghost. Mostly because he could just disappear at will.

I dropped a spoon. "Argh, I'm going to fill this dishwasher back up before I get it emptied. And so what if he does have wild hair and wolfish eyes? Maybe that's exactly what I'm looking for in a man. Oops." I peered up at his face.

His image sharpened and he looked intrigued. "Ah ha, so he is courting you. Going to a play with a friend indeed."

The dogs barked and ran toward the front door.

"He's here, so move along." I waved him away with a flutter of my fingers. "And don't say anything. Twice, Jackson has heard you."

"That's impossible. It was just his imagination."

"Even the British accent?"

"I told you I don't have an accent. You have an accent."

"Not going to get into that silly argument again." I shoved the dishwasher rack into place and closed it. I smoothed my dress and pinched my cheeks. "Go a-way. Now." I headed out of the kitchen.

Newman and Redford sat with tails wagging waiting to greet their visitor. My usual flock of butterflies did their impromptu dance around my belly as I approached the entry. I was hoping to get out the door quickly to avoid any unwanted disturbances from a certain tenant, but Jackson seemed to have different plans.

"I'll just get my coat," I told him as I opened the door. He was wearing a winter coat over a dark blue sweater. It seemed he'd run a brush through his *wild* hair.

He stepped into the entry and patted both dogs. "I was hoping to see the progress you've made." It dawned on him then that I was trying to hurry out the door. "Or I can stay on the porch and wait for you."

"No, don't be silly. I was just rushing so we can get good seats."

"Already took care of that. Sometimes the job comes with perks. We're right up front."

"Oh my, the VIP section. Hope I dressed right." He grabbed my hand as I turned to fetch my coat.

I spun back to him.

He made a long, slow point of looking at my boots. "You look great, and I'm a big fan of those boots."

I turned my foot side to side as if showing off my ankle. "Do you like them? I confess, I bought them on a whim. I hardly ever wear them because they're so impractical. Unless, of course, I'm planning to ride a horse. Although, I've been told these heels would not be practical in stirrups."

"Wouldn't need any spurs, that's for sure."

I paused for a second and had to contain a laugh. He sounded just like Edward. "Do you ride?" I motioned for him to follow me to the dining room, a room that was finally starting to look inhabitable.

"Basically grew up on my grandfather's farm. He had lots of horses. Some well-trained, some not so well-trained. Of course, that never stopped me from climbing on their backs." He reached up and rubbed the back of his head. "I've got a nice scar on my skull to prove just how stupid I was."

We stepped into the dining room. I made my way around the tools and supplies to the work lamp Henry had set up for working late. I flicked it on. It was a harsh, yellowish light, yet Jackson managed to look as if he'd just stepped out of a men's fashion catalog.

"The wainscoting and crown moulding will be painted white. I haven't yet decided on a color for the walls."

Jackson looked around at the room. Ursula and Henry had

done a great job smoothing the walls and the ceilings after everything had been patched. "The Rices are kind of irritating, but they do good work," he said. "It's going to be really nice, Sunni."

"Thank you. It's a lot of work and money, but I think it'll be worth it in the end." I turned off the light. We stood for the briefest moment, just a pair of shadows in a dark room. I could still feel him looking at me though, and it made my cheeks warm.

I led him out of the room. "It's nice that you spent so much time with your grandfather," I said as he followed me to the kitchen.

"Didn't have much choice. Both my parents worked, and I tended to get into trouble when I wasn't supervised. So every summer, they shipped me off to work and play on my grandpa's farm. I had fun and also managed to get in trouble there too. As evidenced by the scar on the back of my head."

We reached the kitchen. I took a quick peek around but saw no sign of Edward. Maybe, for once, he'd actually heeded my request to disappear. Though I was certain he was lingering within earshot of our conversation.

"I'll just grab my coat, and we can be off." As I left the room, Jackson's phone rang.

His deep voice floated through the kitchen as he answered it. "Hey, Trina, can I call you back?"

The woman's name made me trip on the long toe of my boot as I headed down the hallway. I stepped into my room feeling slightly discombobulated. Why had he answered if he knew it was another woman? And why was he making no effort to hide that it was someone named Trina? And are Trina's generally pretty?

I took my time getting my coat from the closet and managed to catch snippets of his conversation.

"We can talk about this tomorrow," he said. "I'm just heading out to the festival with a friend."

Well, that defined my position for the evening. I was a friend and not a date. I pulled the coat on, all the while chastising myself for getting worked up about it. None of it should have been a surprise. He never said the word date, and I certainly knew he had many women friends. I stopped for a second and drew in a breath. It wasn't worth ruining the night over.

Jackson was just hanging up as I stepped into the kitchen. I forced a smile as I buttoned my coat.

"I just noticed you don't have a Christmas tree," he commented as we headed to the front door.

"Not this year. There's just too much happening in the house. Decorating around the clutter seems sort of laughable. I know, I'm a Scrooge."

"No, you're not. Just seems like if it's your first year here, you should put up a tree."

I locked the door behind us. "Now I definitely feel like Ebenezer. Speaking of Scrooge, the man playing the part, Evan Weezer—"

Jackson grunted at the sound of his name. "That guy is always in the middle of things."

"I can tell but that's not what I was going to say. He matches the character so much it's as if Dickens himself created Evan Weezer right off a story page."

"I can see what you mean. He's chewed out officers who were enforcing rules about where realty and open house signs can be posted. Can't tell you how often he's come barreling into the station, nostrils flaring, because his signs had been confiscated."

"Maybe this play will help him see the error of his ways and turn him warm and fuzzy like the fictional Scrooge," I said with a laugh.

The breeze blowing off the mountains carried the scent of snow with it. I pulled the collar of my coat up higher, but it did little to block the chill.

"Hope you don't mind driving to town in my work car. I'm on call. We're still short people. At this rate, it looks like we'll be short all the way through the holidays." He opened the passenger door and I climbed inside.

Jackson slid into the driver's seat and started the engine. He fidgeted with the dials. "Unfortunately, the heater isn't great in here."

"That's all right. It's a short drive." I sat back and debated whether or not to ask about the phone call from Trina. It would probably chew at me all night, but I decided to let it go.

CHAPTER 13

The curtains were still drawn on the stage. They fluttered back and forth with the crew's frenetic activity backstage.

People had marked their seats with hats and gloves but everyone milled about, chatting with neighbors and friends. It took a good twenty minutes for heads to stop turning our direction after Jackson and I arrived at the play. I received a scrutinizing look from more than one woman, but eventually, the curious glances faded and people got back to their own business.

"Sunni," Emily called across the rows of chairs. She waved for us to join them. Nick was wearing a fuzzy red Santa hat, and Emily had pulled on a green and white striped beanie. Lana was standing nearby talking to Mom and Chris.

Mom spotted us and added her enthusiastic wave to the mix. "Sunni, over here," she called.

I kept a smile on my face as I spoke from the corner of my mouth. "Did I mention my family would be here? Please tune out if my mom starts talking about my childhood or teen years or anything in between or after."

"So all topics are off limits?" he asked. "I confessed to you that my parents had to ship me off to my grandfather's farm every summer just to keep me out of trouble."

"Yes, but somehow that only makes you cooler. The stories that my mom hangs onto make me the premier nerdy tomboy."

"I happen to like nerdy tomboys." Jackson said just as we reached the group.

Mom was wearing a chunky bracelet with red and green baubles. She'd added a silver bow clip to her hair. She hugged me and then instantly reached to hug Jackson. He didn't seem to mind.

Mom turned to my sister. "Lana, you need to find two more chairs so Sunni and Brady can sit with us."

Lana held out her purse. "Not sure if I brought along extra chairs but I'll check."

Mom waved off her sarcasm. "I'm sure we can ask the people sitting in our row to move over."

"It's all right, Mom," I said. "We've got our seats already."

Chris pulled away from his conversation with Emily and came toward us. "You must be the detective Maggie was talking so animatedly about this afternoon when we toured the town. Chris Burner, nice to meet you."

"Brady Jackson, nice to meet you."

Chris smiled at me. "Your sister tells us we're in for a treat tonight. Looking forward to it. Can't remember the last time I attended a live play."

"I know they've been working hard to put on a nice production." I thought about my article and how incredibly dull it would read, like a long list of advertisements. In a way, I was almost glad not to be working on a lengthy article. It was sort of like taking a holiday from work. Hopefully, the play would go off without a hitch so I could just fill in specific details about the cast and crew and send it off to Parker.

Mom squeezed between Chris and me. "I was just telling your sister about this gorgeous brooch I saw at a local pawn shop. Lawson's or something like that."

"Larson's Pawn Shop on Butternut Crest?" I asked.

"That's the one. What a cute name for the road too. The brooch was antique. It was in the shape of a sunflower and the yellow petals were made from amber." Mom smiled up at Jackson. "I thought about Brady's unique eye color when I saw it." I nearly sank to the ground in embarrassment, but Jackson just smiled. I was sure it wasn't the first time someone had mentioned his *unique* eye color.

"I tried to buy it for her," Chris interjected.

Mom turned and patted his cheek. "Far too extravagant a gift. Besides, we were just window shopping. Oh look, Nick has some cups of hot cider. I think I'll have one. My face is so cold. It's certainly a blustery night." As if on cue, the canvas panels of the tent dipped down, then billowed out. "I hope this thing holds," Mom laughed and hurried off to get her cider.

Chris moved closer to me. He had tossed a thick gray scarf around his neck which hid his chin. He pushed it down with his fingers so I could hear his lowered voice. "I bought the brooch while she was busy looking at vintage record albums. Unfortunately, I couldn't sneak it into my pocket before she lost interest in the records. Do you think you might have a chance to pick it up for me?"

"Of course. I'll swing by the pawn shop tomorrow. She'll be so excited, Chris."

"I hope so."

Scottie's voice suddenly blurted through a megaphone. "Please start making your way to your seats. We are about to start the play."

"We'll see you guys later," I said just a touch too eagerly.

We said our good-byes, and Jackson and I made our way around the people and chairs to the front row.

"I'm feeling very important right now," I said as we sat down. "Like I've got first class tickets on an airplane."

"I don't know if I'd go that far, but it is nice to sit up front. Only, I'm kind of tall." He turned around to the couple sitting behind us. I recognized the man as one of the pharmacists from the local drug store. "Can you both see the stage well enough around my big head?" Jackson asked.

The woman laughed cheerily. "We can see just fine. Thank you for asking, Detective Jackson." Her tone was practically gushing.

Jackson turned back around, and we settled in for the play. The clamor and voices behind the curtains had quieted. The only sound was the occasional stretching of the canvas as the outdoor elements played drums on the tent.

Quite an elaborate stage had been set up for the performance. The center stage area where the actors would say their lines was highlighted by warm glowing lights. Heavy dark blue curtains concealed the stage and would no doubt be closed during set changes. There were two side entrances onto the main stage, one from each end. Those areas were also hidden by a layer of curtains. A small high school orchestra had been arranged just off to the right of the stage. They were anxiously checking their music and instruments before the curtain went up.

Jackson leaned his head over. "The only thing bad about up front seats is it will be hard to leave during the middle if the play is bad."

"That's true. Let's hope old Evan Weezer Scrooge delivers. Maybe that way he can redeem himself some for terrible behavior."

"He seems nice," Jackson said.

I snapped my face his direction. "I thought you said he comes into the station angry about his signs."

"No, yes, I mean Weezer is terrible. Sorry. I guess I should have prefaced that. Your mom's friend, Chris. He seems like a nice guy."

"I suppose he could be worse. He could be like Weezer."

Jackson shook his head at my tiny concession. "He went out of his way to buy her the brooch she wanted," he noted.

"That's true."

The orchestra started up a melancholy tune and the curtains parted. The audience murmured about the nice set decorations. Bob Cratchit sat at a table, bent over a ledger, trying to read it by the light of a candle nub. The curtains fluttered on the left side of the stage, and Ebenezer Scrooge walked out.

We relaxed back to enjoy the show.

CHAPTER 14

$\mathcal{A}$s scene one concluded, the curtains rolled shut and the breeze outside rattled the tent enough to knock over a few of the cardboard backdrops. The backstage crew hurried to save them from damage, but I could hear Scottie yelling for someone to get the black paint.

In the first act, Ebenezer revealed his nasty, greedy character. I had to admit Evan Weezer did a pretty good job. He certainly upstaged Bob Cratchit, or Nevin Graham, the local jeweler, who kept forgetting his lines and mumbled the ones he remembered.

Jackson stretched out his long legs and slouched down some. He leaned his head over and his thick hair brushed my cheek. "I'm no theater critic," he said, "but Weezer was good in his role. Or maybe it just seemed like it because Graham couldn't remember his lines. When he tripped over the leg of the table, I thought he was going to land in our laps."

"I have to agree, Weezer nailed his part. But then maybe it wasn't such a big stretch for him to get into character." I glanced around and my gaze locked with my mom's all the way across the tent and through a sea of moving heads and shoulders. She winked and waved. I waved back.

"My mom just found us with her mother laser beam. I wonder if she's watching the play or watching us."

Jackson elbowed me lightly. "Guess I won't try any hanky panky with ya if Mom's watching."

I laughed. "Probably a good idea since we are up front and everyone behind us is well aware that the tall head sitting in the front row is none other than the town's detective. And just what kind of hanky panky are we talking about?" I peered over at him.

A teasing smile crossed his face. "I've got a number of tricks up my sleeve."

"I'll bet you do." It was the most flirtatious moment we'd had in a long time and to think it had all been spurred on by my mom. Ugh, that just took the red hot spark out of it.

A sharp wind gust collapsed and puffed the tent like a ship's sail. A few gasps made their way around the audience. An equal amount of gasps flew up from behind the curtain.

"I think they're going to have more trouble with that wind than they realized," I said. "The set was damaged during dress rehearsal too. But it feels like it's getting sort of rough out there."

"I think it might snow later. It's definitely stay close kind of weather." He shifted on his seat and placed his arm around my shoulder. I stiffened for a second, stunned by his move, but then quickly relaxed, stealing some of the nice heat rolling off of him.

Things backstage seemed to be getting more chaotic, but out in the audience, at least in the front row, things were moving along smoothly. With the exception of my suddenly erratic heartbeat.

The audience grew somewhat restless. The curtains split and Scottie stuck her head out. There was a smudge of black paint across her forehead. She looked beyond frazzled. "Play a Christmas song," she barked hoarsely at the orchestra, which was also getting restless.

"Which one?" the boy with the cello asked.

"Oh my gosh, Darren, can't you see I'm busy? Just pick one." She disappeared back behind the curtain.

"Poor Scottie," I said, all the while resisting the temptation to lean my head against Jax. "She's worked so hard on this. Gave up her winter break and everything. After talking to her a few times, I got the sense that she likes everything to be perfect." The audience grew louder. "Although, she might be wise to just leave the damaged sets and get on with the next scene."

"I'm just waiting for the first rotten tomato to come sailing over our heads," Jackson said. His phone buzzed in his pocket. He pulled it out and glanced at it before putting it back into his coat.

I wasn't sure what compelled me to ask the question I'd talked myself out of asking just an hour earlier but it spurted right out before I could rethink it. "Who's Trina?"

"Trina?" he repeated. "That's right, she called while I was in the kitchen. She's one of the clerks at the station. We're paying her overtime to do some filing of old evidence. Her dad lost his job recently, and they're having a hard time of it."

I felt my cheeks darken as he leaned his head over to look at me. "Were you jealous, Bluebird?"

I scooted on the chair and sat up higher. "Nope, just curious." I was saved by an announcement that the show was about to begin again.

Jackson took his arm down so he could scoot lower on the seat and not block the view of people behind him. I was sorry to lose that extra layer of warmth.

The curtains slowly opened revealing the interior of Scrooge's dark, dismal house. My stomach knotted as I realized it looked a little like the inside of the inn. Not a holiday decoration in sight. Somewhere off stage, a clock chimed. It seemed Scrooge was about to climb into bed and be woken by a midnight visit from the ghost of his dead partner, Jacob Marley.

The audience fell silent. The orchestra played a quiet, ominous tune, letting all of us know that the story was about to take a grim turn. The long pause seemed unplanned as we waited silently for some kind of action on stage.

The curtains on the left stage entrance fluttered and moved erratically. A figure stepped through. Evan Weezer was wearing a long sleeping cap and a night tunic as he stepped slowly onto the stage.

Jackson stiffened next to me and sat forward. "Something's not right," he muttered.

He'd barely finished the last word when Evan Weezer fell lifeless and face first toward the stage. Jackson was out of his chair and up the steps before the first screams erupted.

CHAPTER 15

I shot up the steps to the stage, hoping to help with the commotion. Ironically enough, through the horrified, stunned ruckus, just outside the tent someone's phone went off with a merry version of *Jingle Bells*. It sounded so out of place, yet the evening had started as a holiday town event. Only now the merriness had taken a dark turn. I caught a glimpse of Evan's body as Jackson crouched down next to him to search for a pulse. Blood covered the back of his sleeping gown and a long metal object jutted out from his back.

The audience members were on their feet. Pale, shocked faces were locked toward the stage. My gaze shot toward the seats where my family had been seated. Mom had her face hiding against Chris's shoulder, and Nick held Emily and Lana under each arm. The woman, who had sat behind us, sank to her knees and her husband was waving his hand in front of her face to revive her.

"Shut the curtains," I yelled. "Shut them quickly." The crew and actors were in too much shock to understand my simple command. I raced over to the ropes and pulleys and drew the curtains shut to block the scene from the horrified audience.

However, the people backstage had an unobstructed view. Several people raced off looking as if they might throw up. Others followed, no longer wanting to see the grisly sight. The sets that Scottie had taken so much care to paint were broken and bent and tossed around like garbage as people hurried to get off stage.

"Everyone, remain calm," Scottie sobbed and then grabbed the curtain rope to keep herself from collapsing.

Jackson was on the phone calling for backup. I walked over and he peered up at me. "He's dead," he said quietly. "And unless he somehow fell backward on a tent stake, it wasn't an accident."

I looked down at the rod of metal jutting out from the night shirt. "The tent stake." I looked at Jackson. "When I was here on Tuesday, I was talking to some of the cast members and the back corner"—I pointed to the left, rear corner of the tent—"it broke free. It caused quite an uproar. It wasn't easy to catch the ends. It took several of us to hold it in place while someone found another spike. The original one was gone. No one could find it."

Jackson stared down at the body. "Looks like that mystery's been solved." He turned to the remaining people on stage. Scottie was among them, being comforted by Danny Danforth. He was still dressed in costume but had pulled the holly wreath from his head.

"Are you in charge of these people?" Jackson asked Scottie.

She was so shaken, I thought she might crumble at his question. She'd worked so hard to make it a night to remember. Well, she'd succeeded in that. I doubted anyone would forget this evening's play . . . ever.

"This is Scottie Sherman," Danny spoke up for her, since she seemed incapable of responding.

Jackson nodded. "Danny Danforth, right?" he asked.

"Yes, I own Danforth Realty. You probably recognized me from the signs. Although I'm not usually wearing a beard or a big robe." Danny didn't sound the least bit distressed by the murder but then he and Evan weren't exactly buddies.

Jackson glanced around at the stunned faces and moved closer to Danny. "If I could get both of you to clear the stage but have everyone wait. I'm going to need to question everyone to find out if anyone saw what happened to Mr. Weezer."

"Absolutely, Detective Jackson," Danny said.

"Was he murdered?" Scottie squeaked hoarsely. She saw me standing nearby and hurried to me. Her hands were shaky and cold as she grasped my arm. "This is such a disaster. I've been worried about so many silly things going wrong with this play but murder . . ." She released my arm and covered her mouth to stifle another sob.

I placed my arm around her. "I think it might be best for you to go outside and wait with the others. The brisk, fresh air will do you a world of good."

"Miss Taylor, maybe you could help them clear the stage," Jackson said. "I'm going to search the stage area."

I looked his direction. He instantly read my expression of disappointment.

"It would really be a help to me," he said with a pleading pair of amber eyes.

"Yes, of course."

I helped Danny and Scottie corral the last few bystanders, and we walked them out the back exit of the tent. Cold night air splashed all of us out of our stunned stupors. Evan's assistant Tim stood with everyone else looking properly dumbstruck. Tim and the rest of the cast and crew had gathered between the tent and the two trailers that had been brought in for the play. I remembered that Evan Weezer had brought in his own trailer, deciding, apparently, that he was too big of a star to fraternize with everyone else.

I had every intention of slipping right back into the tent to join Jackson for the stage search, but I hung around for a moment to make sure everyone knew they were to stay on site until Jackson could talk to them. Cast members decided to get out of costume and makeup because for most their regular clothes provided more protection from the cold.

Scottie had regained some of her composure. She and Danny seemed to have things under control. The arcing red glow of police and emergency lights lit up the night sky on the street side of the tent. It wouldn't be long before the evidence team and coroner started their work. I wanted to give the stage a once over before the action started.

Evan's body lay motionless in front of the stage entrance curtains, the place he took his last step. Jackson's heavy footsteps echoed on the hollow stage floor behind the curtains. I circled around them to the side stage and found him stooped down taking a picture of something on the floor.

He glanced up momentarily before returning to his task. "How am I not surprised to see you back here, Bluebird? Is everyone settled outside of the tent?"

I moved closer but he put up his hand to stop my progress. "Watch out. There's a trail of blood on the floor. I need to get pictures of it undisturbed. It will tell us the exact path Evan took and, hopefully, the precise location where someone stabbed him with the tent stake. Judging from the diameter of that stake, it couldn't have been too far away. Death would come pretty fast."

"Everyone is settled. Some of the initial horror has faded, but shock is setting in and it's pretty darn cold out there for people who have just gone through something traumatic," I added.

"Yes, I'll get out there in a minute. I'm just waiting for the coroner and evidence crew to get here."

"I saw red lights, so I think they've arrived." I moved cautiously to the place where he had been stooped over taking pictures. A footprint of black paint stained the floor just feet from the place where Evan stepped through. "Do you think it belongs to the killer?" I asked.

"Not sure." Jackson straightened. "There's a puddle of black paint in front of the backdrop. Must have happened during that scene change when the set fell over."

I snapped my fingers only to realize they were too cold to produce sound. "Scottie yelled for someone to get the black paint during the middle of the intermission."

Jackson moved slowly along the stage. "The footsteps start at the puddle and then circle back and fade away as the paint wore off. There are traces of what appears to be black paint on the bottom of the victim's shoes, but there is also a lot of blood. These prints seem to be purely paint. We'll have to get a sample to make certain. But there is one obvious detail about the shoe prints that makes me certain they don't belong to the victim."

I looked down at the one below me. It was so clear it was as if someone had painted it there. "These prints are from giant shoes."

"Massive," he said. "Whoever stepped in the black paint must have been wearing size—"

"Fifteen," I filled in the blank. "Danny Danforth. He told me his feet were size fifteen."

"That's the person I was picturing in my head. I guess I'll start with him."

Voices rumbled through the front of the tent. "I think the coroner is here. I'll get them started and be right out. Tell everyone I'm on my way. Don't want them to get cold feet and leave before I have a chance to talk to everyone. From the trail of blood, it seems Weezer was stabbed just outside the tent or right as he stepped into the side entrance. Could have been anyone backstage."

"That doesn't narrow the field down much, does it?"

"Not really. And I think he had quite a few enemies. Now we just have to figure out who hated him the most."

I felt the smile on my cold face but couldn't stop it. "You know how much I love it when you say 'we' in the middle of an investigation."

He chuckled. "You're easy to please, Bluebird."

CHAPTER 16

*J*ackson held a few interviews in a group setting, just asking general questions about people's locations during the scene change. He asked if anyone saw Evan Weezer before he went on stage. He was able to conclude that Evan had gone to his trailer between scenes. He needed to change out of his Victorian frock coat and top hat and into his nightshirt and cap. His assistant Tim had helped with the costume change.

The bitter temperature outside prompted Jackson to excuse everyone except Tim, Danny, Scottie and a few other cast and crew members who might have seen or heard something significant. The remaining few decided to go inside the makeup trailer to keep warm while they waited for their individual interviews. Jackson complained that it wasn't ideal to have them wait together but there were few other places for them to get out of the elements, and the tent was filled with official activity.

Danny paced along the back of the tent while talking on the phone, retelling the entire harrowing night to someone on the other end. Jackson waved at him to let him know they needed to talk.

Danny hung up from the conversation and walked over. He was fairly jovial considering he'd just witnessed a man's murder. He'd changed out of his Ghost of Christmas Present costume, but there were still remnants of beard glue on his wide chin. He kept scratching at it as if it irritated him.

"I knew you'd be starting with me, Detective Jackson," he said with slight amusement.

It was rare to see Jackson have to turn his face up to look at someone, but Danny was several inches taller. "Why is that, Danforth?"

"Everyone knows that Weezer and I were enemies."

"Were you?" I had no doubt Jackson knew why, but he waited for Danny to explain.

"Look, I'm sorry he's dead. Terrible end for anyone but that guy has been a thorn in my side for years. My realty business was number one. Then Weezer started using every underhanded trick he could find, even going so far as to malign my reputation as an honest broker. It's pretty hard to stand by and watch a scammer make his way to the top when you've been doing everything by the book. Real life is never like the movies. It seems far too often, the bad guys win."

"So, in your eyes, Weezer was the bad guy?" Jackson asked.

"Let's just say no one was shocked that he was picked for the role of Scrooge." Danny shifted on his big feet. He was pretending to act casual, unaffected by the interview, but his fidgety dance told another story. "I didn't like the guy," Danny continued. "I might have occasionally daydreamed about a realty sign blowing off its post and taking off his head or a tree falling through his bedroom window and crushing him but I didn't kill him."

Jackson nodded. "I appreciate your honesty." He dropped his

focus to Danny's shoes. "Can you explain how you got black paint on your shoes?"

"Black paint?" Danny leaned over and lifted the toes of his shoes off the frozen ground. "I didn't know I had any paint on my shoes. I need to find somewhere to sit and take them off. I don't want my socks to get wet."

"You don't need to." Jackson crouched down next to the shoes. They were black to begin with, but it was easy to see the black paint smeared along the toes. Jackson rubbed his finger along the smear and pushed back to standing. He showed proof of the black paint.

"There's an easy explanation," Danny said. "There was some damage to one of the sets after the first scene. And Scottie, who is a perfectionist, called someone to bring black paint and repair the damage. In the confusion backstage, the paint got spilled. And with my big boats—" He rocked his feet back and forth. "I managed to step right into it. I don't see how paint on my shoes is relevant."

Jackson pulled out his phone to show the photos he'd taken of the shoe print. Danny pulled a pair of reading glasses out of his coat pocket and squinted at the picture. "Yep, I'd say there's only one person who could leave that kind of print. Unless Bigfoot wandered down from the mountains," he added with a laugh. Danny certainly wasn't going to let the somber event ruin his evening.

"That shoe print was taken right next to the curtain at the left hand stage entrance, the place where Evan stepped through before dying on stage."

Danny's jovial grin, a remnant of his Bigfoot joke, faded. His mouth flattened, and his expression grew more serious. "That still doesn't mean I killed him."

"No one's saying that," Jackson said calmly. "If you can just explain what you were doing behind that particular set of curtains. I've seen enough versions of *A Christmas Carol* to know there were still several scenes before the Ghost of Christmas Present made an appearance."

Danny's mouth pulled in. It seemed he was trying to come up with a reason for being at the stage entrance at that time. He pulled out a tissue to wipe his red, cold nose and to stall for time. Then he pushed the tissue back into his pocket. "I guess I might as well confess."

Jackson and I both stood up straight as if someone had just poked us.

Danny seemed to realize his words were alarming. "Not a confession to murder," he said quickly, once again needing the tissue for his nose. "My goodness, certainly not that." He finished with his nose again and took a deep breath. A puffy white cloud appeared in front of his face. "I wanted to throw Evan off his game. He was in his trailer getting changed for the scene. While everyone was busy repairing the set, I found a hiding place in the heavy curtains. I wasn't going to do anything terrible. Just, you know—" His gaze dropped back to the big shoes. "Just stick my toe out as he walked on stage. I thought if I planned it right, he'd land right on his bony knees in front of the whole town, nightshirt and all." He looked somewhat contrite after saying it aloud. "Just his knees. Who knew he'd end up falling face first instead."

"If you were hiding in the curtains," Jackson started, but Danny shook his head.

"Didn't see a thing. While I was trying to stay tucked away out of sight, not an easy feat at my size, I caught a glimpse of Scottie. She was rushing around in such a frenzy, trying to get everything on stage just right, I didn't have the heart to go through with it. I didn't want to let her down. So I stepped out of my hiding spot and left the stage area completely. I never saw Weezer walk in."

"You didn't see anyone hanging around, maybe someone who shouldn't have been there at all?"

Danny rubbed his chin, stopping to scratch some of the beard glue off. "Just the crew and they were all busy helping with the set."

Jackson looked toward the trailer where the others had taken shelter. "Can you think of anyone who hated Weezer enough to kill him?"

His booming, short laugh got lost in the cold night air. "He was a pretty despicable guy. There are plenty of us in the real estate world who were hoping for his downfall. But I don't know anyone who is capable of murder."

"Detective Jackson." The coroner's assistant came around the tent. "We need you inside. The victim's fiancée just arrived at the scene."

"I'll be right there," Jackson said.

"She's very distraught," the woman added. "She burst into the tent. We hadn't covered the victim yet."

Jackson nodded. "Well, cover him now. I'll be right there." He turned back to Danny. "Thank you, Mr. Danforth. You've been helpful. I might still have questions for you, but you're free to go for tonight."

Danny lumbered away with his painted shoes.

"May I tag along? It's getting kind of chilly out here." I rubbed my hands together and pushed them into my coat pockets.

"Probably a good idea for you to step into the tent and warm up. Wouldn't want that button nose of yours to pop off in the cold."

I reached up to touch my nose. "It no longer has feeling. If it did pop off, I probably wouldn't notice."

We headed to the side opening on the tent. "I'm just an amateur, of course," I said. "But I thought his blatant honesty about how much he despised Evan, even admitting to dreaming about his demise, made him seem more innocent. It seems like the real killer wouldn't be so free with his feelings. Without giving away any of your special, top secret detective knowledge, am I right with my theory? Or at least close?"

"Well, I don't want to divulge anything top secret," he said with a wink "but I'd say you've got pretty good instinct for an amateur. But that doesn't let him off the hook yet. His highly recognizable footprint puts him close to the scene at the time of the murder. That means he stays on my person of interest list."

Jackson held open the flap of the tent and I walked inside. A woman's sobs rolled toward us.

"Who knew there was a fiancée?" Jackson muttered.

"A better question might be—how on earth did Evan Weezer Scrooge win a woman's heart?" I whispered back.

CHAPTER 17

*E*ven though Evan's highly distraught fiancée was on her knees and bent over the body, which was now, thankfully, draped in the coroner's sheet, I recognized her instantly as the young woman who had been setting up the Nativity manger at the other end of the festival.

"Who would have done something so horrible?" she asked to no one in particular.

The coroner, an older woman with frizzy gray hair and thick glasses seemed more than pleased to see Jackson.

"Detective Jackson, this is the deceased's fiancée, Joanna Fritz," the coroner said with a tilt of her head. "I assume you need to talk to her." She added a brow raise that silently told him to please take the woman aside so their work could get done.

Jackson walked over to her. "Miss Fritz," he said quietly. "Maybe we could move to the audience chairs and have a talk."

Joanna lifted her face. Instantly, I was reminded of the day before when I saw her setting up the manger. Her eyes and nose were puffy and red then too. I was convinced she'd been crying.

Jackson held out his hand. She took it and he helped her to her feet. She swayed a little bit.

"Can I get you some water or a hot tea?" I asked.

"No, thank you," she said weakly. "I couldn't ingest anything right now."

Joanna's legs wobbled as Jackson led her cautiously down the stage steps to the center of the tent where the rows of chairs, once set in perfect lines like crops in a field, were now jumbled into disarray. A few knit hats and the occasional lone glove had been left behind during the abrupt evacuation.

Jackson picked several chairs far enough from the stage to avoid hearing any discussion between the coroner and her assistants. Joanna reached for the gloves in her pocket. "I'm sorry, my hands are cold. Must be the shock." Her voice wavered as she spoke, but she had calmed down considerably on the short journey to the chairs. Her fingers trembled slightly as she pulled on the gloves. Oddly enough, there was no engagement ring on her finger, only a slight depression in the skin as if one had been there not long before. I was sure a boastful, successful man like Evan Weezer would have been the type to buy his intended a large, showy diamond ring. But then I had witnessed him being incredibly stingy with his assistant, wanting back a quarter for change. Maybe he'd been too cheap to buy a nice ring, or maybe it was being fitted better. It was possible Joanna had left it somewhere safe at home while she worked on the festival Nativity scene.

"I understand you and Mr. Weezer were going to be married," Jackson said after waiting for her to put on gloves and settle on her chair.

She hesitated rather dramatically before answering. "Yes, yes we were. We had big plans for the future," she said with a shuddering sigh, one that seemed forced.

"Were you at the play tonight?" Jackson asked.

"No, I couldn't attend." She turned and stared sadly up at the activity on stage. Several police officers were still combing the set for evidence. She turned back to Jackson. "I still can't believe it," she said.

"I'm sure this has been a tremendous shock, Miss Fritz," Jackson wrote down her name on his notes. "Are there next of kin we should be contacting?"

She shook her head. "Evan wasn't in contact with any family members. His parents live abroad, and he hasn't spoken to his brothers in years. But I can get word to all of them." She pressed her arm against her stomach. "I'm not feeling too well, I'm afraid."

"That's understandable. I'll keep it brief. Could you tell me where you were during the play? And how did you hear about—" He paused for the right words, but there wasn't any particular way to sugarcoat it. "How did you learn about Mr. Weezer's death?"

Her mouth pursed some, and she shifted stiffly on the chair. It was always interesting to see people's reactions to questions that were slightly accusatory. Danny had taken it in stride, even expecting to be considered a suspect since he and Evan were enemies, but Joanna hadn't anticipated it at all. "I'm in charge of the festival Nativity scene. I had to be there tonight because the live animals, a burro and a goat, had been brought in for the display. It gets pretty hectic, with people wanting to take pictures and all. People try and climb into the display to take selfies with the wise men." She shook her head slightly. "I stayed around to make sure they didn't ruin the display. It takes me a good, long while to set it up just right." She still hadn't answered his question.

"How did you find out about Mr. Weezer?" Jackson prodded.

"There was finally a lull in the activity at the Nativity scene when most of the festival visitors left to watch the play. I'd brought a book and thermos of coffee along in my car. I took a break from the cold and sat in my car to read and warm up. I was able to park in a place where I could still keep an eye on the Nativity scene and the animals. I didn't know anything had happened until several emergency vehicles sped past. I climbed out of the car and met a large swarm of people heading down the sidewalk away from the theater tent. I saw a few women I knew. Angie, a neighbor of mine, looked close to throwing up. She tried to avoid me, but I caught up to her and asked her what happened. She finally blurted the terrible news and hurried away. I stood frozen in shock for a few minutes, not sure whether to believe the news. Not wanting to believe it. When I finally gathered my wits, I raced for the tent." She covered her mouth to stifle a sob. "It was like a terrible nightmare coming true."

The coroner's gurney had been moved to the stage steps. The group working on stage was trying to figure out whether to bring the body down or the gurney up. I shot a horrified look at Jackson. Whatever course of action they chose, it didn't seem like something the grieved fiancée should have to witness.

Jackson stood up. "Miss Fritz, do you have someone to see you home? I could ask one of the officers to escort you or at least take you to your car."

She shook her head weakly. "Frankly, I think the walk in the fresh air will do me good. My stomach is upset, and my head is pounding. I have a friend meeting me at home in an hour, so I'll be fine. Thank you."

Jackson offered his hand, which she readily accepted. We were just about to part when Jackson paused. "Miss Fritz, just one more question if you don't mind. You said you were in your car while people attended the play. Was there anyone around who saw you sitting in the car at that time?"

"Well, no, not that I can think of." A short dry laugh followed. "Detective Jackson, you can't think that I had anything to do with this. Evan was my fiancé. We had a bright future together."

"Of course not, Miss Fritz. Just doing my job." He smiled politely at her before walking away.

As we headed back toward the stage something occurred to me.

I placed my hand on Jackson's arm to stop him. "I just remembered something." I glanced back to see that Joanna hadn't followed us. She was just exiting through the front of the tent.

"What is it? Something about Miss Fritz?"

"Yes. Remember when I told you that the corner of the tent had come loose because someone had removed a stake? Well, Miss Fritz was there that day. When Danny Danforth and I rushed over to help them keep control of the tent in the wind, Joanna was there helping out. I didn't know her at the time, only that she was the woman setting up the Nativity scene. Which brings me to another point, but I don't want to get off track from the first point. While we were out there, helping the crew secure the tent, Joanna included, Evan came out of his trailer to see what the commotion was about. He didn't lend a hand or anything. In fact, Danny snidely told him to go back to his trailer for a nap or some other sarcastic suggestion. What's strange is, I was standing right next to Joanna Fritz. I don't recall Evan saying one word to her. There wasn't so much as a smile toward each other. At least not that I noticed. Of course, I wasn't watching for it either. We were all in the middle of holding onto a tent that badly wanted to take off to the sky like a freed balloon."

"Kind of strange that he saw his fiancée helping out but didn't offer to join in. But then, from what you've told me, Weezer wasn't exactly the helpful type. I did wonder about the ring."

"Yes, me too. There was clearly an indentation on her ring finger as if it had been there earlier."

"There might be a perfectly logical reason for that though. There's no real reason for her to make up a story about being his fiancée."

"Detective Jackson," the coroner called down from the stage. "We're going to be moving the body if you're ready to be briefed."

"Yes, I'll be right there." Jackson turned back to me. "What was the second point?"

"Huh?" My mind had been swirling about the reasons for the missing ring. "Oh yes, the second point. The first time I saw Joanna, she was arranging the three wise men in the Nativity manger. She looked then as if she'd been crying. I remember thinking it was sort of strange. She was in the middle of all the decorating and festivities, deep in her task, but her face and eyes were puffy as if something had upset her. The next time I saw her was at the tent incident. It seemed as if she'd recuperated from whatever had upset her earlier in the day."

"Thanks for the scoop. It's always nice to have a little bird flitting around town taking in important details."

"Do you think that might be significant? I was just mentioning it because it seemed odd."

"You never know. Crimes of passion are pretty common. I'm going to head up to the stage and get the low down on all of this. Where are you going to be? There's a murderer on the loose, so don't wander away. Keep close."

"I'll just *flit* around the tent area to see what I can dig up. My *bird's eye view* of things might reveal something your evidence team didn't catch."

"Be careful and if something doesn't look right, don't do anything on your own. Come back here immediately."

I rested my hand on my chest. "Are you suggesting that I might do something dangerous or reckless?" I asked with feigned outrage.

"Do you mean like climb a tree to get a look at a crime scene? Yes, that's exactly what I'm suggesting." His brows lowered, and his amber eyes darkened. He took hold of my hand. His was amazingly warm, but my fingers were nearly numb from the cold. "Sunni, I'm serious. I don't know who the killer is or if they're even still around, but in my years on the force, I've learned that once someone kills, they are far less hesitant to do it a second time."

I smiled. "I'll be careful, Jax. I promise. I won't wander far either. It's too darn cold out there for adventure."

"All right. I'll be done here soon, then I can take you home before those fingers break off. How come you didn't bring any gloves tonight?"

I shrugged and batted my lashes dramatically. "What's the fun of holding hands with someone when you're wearing gloves?"

His grin helped thaw the chill in my bones. He lifted my hand and kissed the back of it. "Hmm, like honey flavored ice cream. I'll see you shortly."

CHAPTER 18

The two officers who had been combing the perimeter of the tent for evidence had finished their work. They'd marked off an area with cones and caution tape just beyond the side entrance. It seemed to be the place where Evan walked into the tent to get to the stage. They had sprayed a thin white line and three dots on the packed dirt. The paint was already trickling away from the cold moisture. A portable light lit up the small area inside the caution tape. I crouched down. The white paint markers made it easy to find the drops of dark blood on the wet ground. A long stream of blood led toward the entrance on the tent.

I followed the yellow tape and lifted the entrance flap. There were more cones and white paint on the ground inside the tent. Apparently, Evan had been stabbed just as he entered the tent for his performance. I returned to the outside cones and looked around. Not long ago, the killer had been standing close to the same spot, waiting to impale Evan Weezer with a tent stake. It had to be someone who truly hated him, someone whose life had been upset so much by Evan, they had waited in the cold, with the entire town just yards away on the other side of the canvas walls.

The lights were still on in both trailers. Yellow caution tape blocked the entrance to Evan's personal trailer. I was sure the forensic team had already done a thorough search of the trailer. Scottie and the few people who had been asked to stay were still sitting in the second trailer, waiting for Detective Jackson. I was sure they were anxious to head home. The play would have just been ending, but I had no doubt they were all exhausted from the terrible shock.

Jackson was still inside being briefed by his team and the coroner. I had a few minutes to kill, so I decided to pull out my handy pen light and do a quick survey around the perimeter of the tent. For the most part, the brittle wind had died down. Earlier in the evening, it had caused enough trouble to push over backdrops by blowing against the tent walls. Since the backdrops fell forward, it was easy to conclude that the wind had been blowing against the back of the tent. That meant anything, loose debris, fabric, even fibers from a fake beard would have been blown across the ground toward the tent. And since the tent was only connected firmly to the ground where stakes held it down, it seemed entirely possible that some of that debris would have been pushed just under the bottom edge of the canvas. It was a large structure, but I didn't need to go much farther than the side entrance where Evan took his last few steps.

I skirted along the edge and lifted the thick hem of the tent with one hand while shining the penlight into the dark space with the other. A chocolate bar candy wrapper was the first thing to flutter out from under the canvas. I stopped it with my toe before it could fly away. I reached into my coat pocket and dug around for the small pack of tissue I kept handy for sneezes, runny eyes from cold winds and any other fiasco requiring tissue. I pulled out a piece and used it to pick up the candy wrapper. I moved along the perimeter and was starting to feel fairly disappointed in my plan when a long, yellow strand of straw rolled out. I picked it up with a new tissue and examined it. It was definitely the straw used in barns and . . . I thought excitedly. Nativity manger scenes.

I glanced around the area. There didn't seem to be any reason for a piece of straw to be stuck under the tent. It had to have been carried there on someone's shoe or clothing. I tucked the straw away gently into the tissue as if it were fragile and irreplaceable. I doubted it would have any significance in the investigation, but I'd learned not to ignore anything that seemed out of place. And the piece of straw sure seemed to be a long way from home, wherever that home might be.

"Sunni?" a familiar voice called across the lot. "Is that you?"

I shaded my eyes against the light pouring through the open door on the trailer. Scottie was standing on the metal steps waving at me.

"Yes, it's me." I tucked my collected treasures into my coat pocket and walked across to the trailer.

Scottie had pulled on a scarf and puffy parka. She held up a mug. "We have coffee and cocoa if you're interested."

I stopped at the bottom step and smiled up at her. "Thank you so much, but I think Detective Jackson is just about done. I'm sorry you all had to wait so long. He should be here soon, so you can all go home."

"Yes, I hope so," Scottie sighed. "I'm going to steep myself in a hot bath like a bag of tea and soak until all of this night is washed away from memory."

"That sounds like a solid plan."

Tim's pale, drawn face poked through the opening. "Will Detective Jackson be excusing us soon? My wife is on her way to pick me up."

"You know what, why don't I go check on that. I think he was just waiting for the coroner to finish." The sound of the word coroner seemed to wash even more color from his face.

"Have they removed—have they taken the body—have they taken Evan away?" Tim's voice was rough and froggy as he stuttered looking for the right phrase.

"I believe that's what they've been doing these past twenty minutes or so. I'll find out and let Detective Jackson know you're all waiting to talk to him."

"Thank you, Sunni," Scottie called as I headed back to the crime scene.

I entered through the back exit, making sure to avoid the area near the yellow caution tape. The space behind the stage was dark and shadowy. As I stepped beneath the flap and lifted my face, I gasped as I ran smack into a large, hard body.

"Bluebird." Jackson sounded nearly as surprised as me. "I was just coming outside." His large hands had curled around my arms to keep me from being knocked back off my feet by the impact. He left them there much longer than needed since I'd clearly regained my balance and composure. (Although his nearness and grasp on my arms nearly made that composure slip away again.)

He released his hold on me, but I was sure I noted some hesitation. "Weezer is on his way to the morgue. I was just heading over to talk to the few witnesses I asked to stay. They're probably ready to throw hot cocoa and gloves at me for making them wait so long."

"I think that might be the case. That's why I was heading in to see you. I'll walk back to the trailer with you. There was an offer of cocoa earlier, and I think I might just take it."

We headed across the lot to the trailer. "Did you find anything interesting while you were out here?" he asked.

"A couple of things, although interesting is a strong word. I'll show you later. Just don't get your hopes up for much. I'm pretty sure they're nothing of value. How about you? Did the forensics team find anything significant?"

"Sure, they found all kinds of evidence. We now know that Evan Weezer was stabbed with a metal stake as he entered the tent."

I looked sideways at him. "I think the entire town knew that."

"Yep. That's about all we've got so far. They found the blood trail and we have a body with the murder weapon. We just haven't found anything that points to the actual killer."

CHAPTER 19

*A*s we reached the steps outside the trailer, headlights lit up the area. Tires crunched the cold ground as a car rolled slowly around to the back of the tent and parked.

Jackson turned toward the car. "Who could this be?"

A woman wearing a bright pink parka and scarf climbed out of the driver's seat. We were the ones stuck in her headlights, but she was the one who paused like a stunned deer. The passenger door opened and a pair of crutches and wrapped ankle appeared. A tall, thin teenage boy with a blue and white striped beanie pulled down low over his head pushed himself out of the car and up onto the crutches. It took him a second to get his balance.

The woman looked over the top of the car. "Timmy, I told you to stay inside the car."

"It's too cold. And I want to see what's going on." Timmy answered.

"That's Tim's wife and his son." I paused to control a grin. "Tiny Tim. I mean Tim Junior. Oh, and look, he's on crutches. Tim works for Evan Weezer and his son who walks on crutches is Tim

Junior." I repeated the whole scenario in case Jackson missed the coincidences.

"Except that Tim Junior isn't the least bit tiny, and Scrooge's mistreated employee was named Bob."

I waved off his corrections. "Phonetic details. The main context is still there."

The senior version of Tim came out of the trailer at the sound of his wife's voice. "Helen, I told you I'd still be a few minutes. You might as well come inside the trailer and have cocoa. I still need to talk to the detective." Tim had pulled on his coat and scarf. "Could you talk to me next, Detective Jackson? As you can see, my son's just recovering from a sprained ankle. That's why they missed the play. Now, I'm thankful they did."

Jackson pulled out his notebook. "I was planning to talk to you next, Mr. Barton. Maybe we could talk out here while your wife and son go inside to get cocoa."

His wife's cheeks were as pink as her parka. She stopped in front of us and looked up at her husband. "So, it's really true? Evan Weezer is dead?"

"I'm afraid so," Jackson said.

"I suppose I'm not too surprised. That man made enemies everywhere he went," she added as she moved past us to climb the stairs. Tim helped his son navigate the few steps up to the trailer.

Jackson turned to me. "Maybe you should get out of the cold too."

"Probably a good idea." I lowered my voice, so only he could hear me. "But stay close to the trailer. The small front window is open. I'm not ashamed to admit I plan on eavesdropping."

"I'm not surprised," he said quietly back.

"Because I'm not ashamed or that I've already hatched a plan to listen in?"

"Both."

"All right, Detective Jackson," Tim said as he trotted down the steps. "I'm all yours. Ask away."

"Excuse me," I said politely and hurried up to the trailer to get a spot near the window.

The small interior of the trailer was warm and steamy from the people and the constant flow of cocoa. A tiny kitchenette stood in the center of the space, acting as a divider between the two makeup and hairstyle stations at the end of the unit and the sitting area at the front.

"There you are, Sunni," Scottie said from her place at the stove. "I just handed your cup of cocoa to Timmy. Poor kid, there's nothing worse than trying to move around on crutches during winter. Did it myself once when I broke three toes skiing. I'm making you a fresh cup now. You look like the whipped cream type," she added.

"I'm absolutely the whipped cream type." I was in luck. A fold out bench was positioned right below the open window. I sat down on it.

"Don't sit there, Sunni. We've got the window open to let some of the steam out," Scottie said. "If you're directly under it, you'll catch a chill."

"That will only make the hot cocoa that much more enjoyable." I smiled at the other cast members, Carly Gomez, the pet shop owner and former Christmas ghost and Hubert Cummings, the funeral home owner who was playing the ghost of Jacob Marley. They looked tired and ready to go home as they clutched their cups of cocoa.

The group was pulled into a discussion about Timmy's injury and their own tales of broken and sprained limbs. I leaned my head back hoping to hear the conversation outside over the cocoa chat club going on inside.

Jackson's voice was deep and smooth, almost too mellow to

carry up to the window, but Tim's voice had a high, agitated pitch to it that sliced cleanly through the crisp night air.

"I helped Evan changed out of his scene one costume and into the night shirt and cap he needed for scene two. He was his usual self, cranky and always snapping his fingers at me to hurry up. A runner came to let us know it was time for him to get back on stage. He walked out of the trailer, and I stayed behind to tidy up. I knew he'd need the frock coat, vest and trousers for future scenes. I hung them up so they'd be ready for a quick costume change."

"Evan's trailer is on the opposite side of the lot, the side where Evan entered the tent. From the pattern of blood outside the entrance, it's also the side of the tent where Evan was stabbed. Did you see anyone on that side when you were in his trailer straightening up?" Jackson asked.

"Here you go," Scottie said. "Complete with whipped cream." She handed me a hot cup that was topped with a swirl of cream. "I put a few mini marshmallows in too," she added.

I smiled and said thank you far too abruptly, but I was missing Tim's answer.

"I'm happy to get rid of some of these goodies. You see I had an after performance cast party planned complete with cocoa and cookies." Scottie pointed at me. "Do you want a cookie? They're iced sugar cookies."

"No, thank you." I lifted the cocoa. "This should be all I need for a proper sugar high."

Scottie laughed. "That's for sure." Thankfully Timmy asked for a refill and Scottie was pulled away. I'd missed some of the exchange, but I was confident Jackson would fill me in if I asked.

"He was a terrible man to work for," Tim's voice drifted toward the open window. "But I have a family to take care of. I figured I would learn a lot about the real estate business if I assisted the number one agent in town. He was demanding and rude and treated me badly, but I was learning tricks of the trade. I was sure if I could stick it out with him, I'd be tougher and far more skilled once I got my license to buy and sell houses. I disliked him more than any person I've ever met, but I would never dream of killing him. Technically, I'm out of a job now. Why would I sabotage my own income?"

"You've been very helpful, Mr. Barton. Here's my card if you can think of anything else I should know. You should probably get your family home now. The temperature is dropping quickly."

Tim climbed up the steps. As he entered the trailer, my phone buzzed with a text from Raine.

"I heard the play was a disaster. I assume the date ended just as abruptly. I'm heading over to Lana's to watch White Christmas with them. I can stop by the inn and pick you up."

I glanced at the remaining cast members who would need to talk to Jackson. It made me yawn with fatigue. Suddenly, a ride home sounded good. I had work in the morning, and it wasn't as if there was any way to hope for a happy ending to our night out.

I texted back. "I'm still in town at the site of the play. Jackson is conducting the investigation. If you wouldn't mind swinging past here, I'll wait out front. And instead of picking me up at the inn, I would love it if you dropped me off there. I'll have to skip Bing Crosby tonight. I'm too tired."

"I can do that," Raine said. "Only if you provide details of the night as we drive back to the inn."

"Not sure there are too many to provide but it's a deal."

Jackson stepped into the trailer and instantly filled the entire space in all his tall, broad-shouldered glory. Carly Gomez was more than happy to step outside for a few questions. The group said their good-byes to Timmy and Susan.

Jackson was handed a cup of hot coffee as he made his way to where I was sitting, finishing my cocoa. "I'll probably be another hour or so," he said with an apologetic curl of his brows.

I stood up. "That's fine. Raine is coming by to pick me up. She'll give me a ride back to the inn. The cocoa warmed me from the inside, but I need a hot shower."

"I'm sorry about all this, Bluebird. It wasn't exactly how I pictured our night out."

"Do you mean you weren't expecting a murder?" I smiled but I was even too tired for a proper one. "You should head home soon too, Detective Jackson. You looked tired."

He lifted the cup of coffee. "Hoping this will give me a jolt."

"I'm going to head out front to wait for Raine."

"I don't want you to go alone. There's a killer on the loose."

I patted his arm. "There are still plenty of people milling about the sidewalks and taking carriage rides. I'll be fine. Get your work done here so you can get home." Just as I finished, we noticed the few people left in the trailer had fallen silent. They watched us with keen curiosity and slight grins.

"Don't let us get in the way of a good night kiss, Detective Jackson," Scottie quipped.

A blush warmed my cheeks, which didn't escape Jackson's notice. That first kiss had eluded us several times. I certainly didn't plan to finally get it in front of an audience standing in a cloud of cocoa steam inside a small trailer.

Jackson pointed out the shiny badge on his belt. "I never kiss while on duty. Miss Gomez, I'll speak to you next if you're ready."

CHAPTER 20

*R*aine was pouting like a fish by the time she dropped me at the inn. There were no juicy date details because our night had been cut short. I didn't have much to add about the murder that Lana hadn't already described in dramatic detail. I was sure there were at least a hundred different accounts of Evan's horrifying death scuttling around town and most of them embellished, like my sister's account. Lana apparently decided that Evan stumbled out into the spotlight, clutching wildly at the stake in his back before falling like a stone on the stage. With an eye roll, I told Raine that I must have looked away when he was struggling to remove the stake and standing in the spotlight.

I thanked her for the ride and sent my apologies along for pooping out on the holiday movie, then headed up the front steps of the inn. I was very much regretting leaving my gloves behind when I tried with icy fingers to get the key in the front lock. In my nervous rush to leave the house with Jackson, I'd also forgotten to turn on the porch light, making my task even harder. When the key slipped from my numb fingers, I was just about to give up, circle around to the back and inch my way through the dog door.

"Darn it." I stooped down to search for the key but once again lack of light and feeling in my fingers were working against me. My fingers finally landed on the key just as the wicker chair on the corner of the porch scraped the floorboards.

I gasped as I shot to standing, the key slipping once again from my fingers. My heart pummeled my rib cage, but the breath, caught in my throat, slowly released as Edward floated into view. He had that faraway, extra transparent look on his face. Without a word, he came closer. He moved by me so closely, he passed partially through me. I shivered as the cold vapor crossed my flesh and bones. He easily retrieved the key and pushed it into the lock. The door opened and he waved me in with a bow.

"Thank you." I bustled past him into the entryway. "I was afraid I'd be out there all night stuck in the nightmarish scenario where I struggled with the lock, dropped the key and then stooped down to pick it up, only to start the cycle all over again."

The front door and lock snapped shut behind me as I traveled down the hallway to the kitchen. The cold had left me with a headache. I was in need of some hot tea.

Edward was on his perch over the hearth as I turned on the kitchen light. The dogs lifted their tired heads and then dropped back into their doggie dreams.

"A gentleman would see a lady to the house and make sure she was safely inside before driving away," Edward said. His scowl looked more miserable than usual.

"That wasn't a gentleman. That was Raine. She gave me a ride home."

"Ah, yes, the woman who talks to ghosts. And that makes your gentleman friend even more of a blackguard. Why didn't he drive you home?"

"He was busy with an investigation. I told you, he's a detective."

I put the kettle on and sat at the table. Edward drifted down and joined me. "We went to the town play. They were acting out *A Christmas Carol.*"

Edward looked puzzled.

"That's right. Charles Dickens was a little after your time." I laughed. "That sounds so strange telling someone that Dickens was after their time."

He didn't look amused.

"What's wrong with you, Edward? You're so grumpy lately."

He pulled a banana out of the fruit bowl and balanced it on his vaporous fingertip. "Not bad," I said. "Of course, it probably helps that you can ignore the law of gravity."

"Gravy?" he asked.

"No, I think we've had this discussion before. I'm too tired tonight. But you haven't answered my question. Is it just the noise in the house?"

Edward tossed the banana back into the bowl. "I suppose that's part of it."

"What's the other part?"

He coasted to the kitchen window and stared out. "As a child, I looked so forward to the first snowfall. The crunch of the ice beneath boots and horse hooves. Flakes landing on your nose and tongue. Then returning to the house to warm myself by the hearth. Olga, our cook, always had a beef pie ready when I came in from the snow."

I walked to the kettle while I listened to him reminisce about being alive just like someone might reminisce about their childhood. But for living people, it was possible to relive the nostalgic memories, to taste and feel and smell the wonders of winter that they remembered from childhood. Edward was bound inside a world without the magic of senses.

"Edward, I'm sorry I've haven't spent any time lately on untangling your reason for being stuck here at the inn. I'm certain it has to do with knowing what happened to your child. I promise first chance I get, I'll return to the records office to see if there is some kind of birth certificate. Now that I know Bonnie's maiden name, it might be easier to find the record."

I filled my teacup.

"Do what you will. I doubt it will make much difference," he grunted.

"Well, bah humbug to you too," I said.

"Bah humbug. Charles Dickens with his ridiculous prose and unlikable characters. He made it seem as if Victorian London was the most wretched, vile place on the map."

"So you do know of him?"

"Mary, the woman whose ludicrous family lived here mid-century used to read those books to her children every night. I told her they would have nightmares and turn into foul adults hearing that nonsense, but she never listened."

"Perhaps because at that time, Dickens was like the rock star of the book world."

"What is a rock star? Someone who shows off rocks?"

"No, they're musicians and singers," I explained and then realized I'd inadvertently trapped myself in one of our endless 'twenty question' sessions.

"These are musicians who use rocks instead of instruments?" Edward asked, predictably.

"No, they play real instruments, but the music is called rock. Rock n' roll to be exact."

Edward's image tightened with interest. At least I'd popped him out of his grumpy mood. "There is music called rock and roll? Does it have anything at all to do with actual rocks? Or rolls, for that matter?"

I smiled at him. "No, no it doesn't. I listen to it on my computer when I'm working."

"Yes, the discordant clamor that makes you wriggle on your

chair. Preposterous name for music." Edward moved back to his place on the hearth. "I think you brought it up just to steer me away from our first topic."

I rubbed my forehead. The tea and warmth of the kitchen was slowly melting the ache away. "You mean your dour mood?" I took another soothing sip of tea. It was a special blend of cinnamon and orange, one of my favorites.

"See, you're doing it again. I'm talking about the lack of manners from your gentleman friend." He huffed. "Although, one can hardly use the term on someone with such a wild appearance. Does the man not own a looking glass or comb?"

"I happen to like his hair. There was no lack of manners on his part. A man was murdered, and the detective was doing his job. And now, I'm going to stand in a hot shower until I'm thoroughly thawed out from the long night. Then I'm going straight to bed."

I stopped on the way out and looked back at him. Occasionally, I caught him in a moment of reflection, and it always made him seem lonely, even a little lost. "If I get time, I'll go back to the records office to see what I can find out about Bonnie's baby."

He shrugged. "Do what you want. Makes no difference to me," he said unconvincingly.

"All right, Edward. Good night."

"Good night, Sunni."

CHAPTER 21

My article about the play had taken an unexpected turn. I'd settled on writing a pedestrian piece about how the business community came together in the holiday season to delight us with their thespian talents. The article would include the obligatory contact information and pleasant write-up about their respective businesses and that would be the end of it. My job for the week would be fulfilled, and Parker would be pleased, all with very little brain energy wasted. But now there was no play to write about. Murder and intrigue were much more interesting to write about, but I had little to go on.

I decided to start with the person who seemed to have the most to gain from Evan's death. With Weezer out of the way, Danny Danforth was sure to have a nice boost in business.

Danforth Realty was a small office just before the Smoky Highway in the town of Hickory Flats. I'd called ahead, and his assistant, Roger, had answered. He told me he expected Danny in any time because he had a meeting with new clients. I let him know I only needed a few minutes of Danny's time and that it was for the newspaper. Which it was, technically. If I happened to gather some helpful information about the murder at the same time, then that would be the cherry on top.

Hickory Flats was a quiet, almost rural kind of town with far less traffic and activity than Firefly Junction. It was also at a lower elevation so the flakes of snow that had fallen the night before had already melted to puddles on the sidewalk.

A mid thirties man with a stylish gray business suit and clean shaven face peered up over the top of his monitor as I walked into the office. The nameplate on his desk said Roger Urban.

"How can I help you?" he asked.

I pulled out my press pass. "I'm Sunni Taylor from the *Junction Times*. I spoke to you this morning about an interview with Mr. Danforth."

"Right. I'm afraid Danny got called away to show some houses. With Evan Weezer—gone," he said politely. "We've been swamped with calls. Even in realty, the show must go on," he quipped and then turned red with embarrassment. His lips pulled in for a second. "I guess that was not the best phrase to use in this situation."

"Probably not. But I suppose it makes sense that Danny will gain a lot of business with his main competitor—gone." I knew it was a leading statement, but I'd lost the morning's interview. I hoped to save it by prying some information out of Danny's assistant. I'd always found assistants to have far more valuable information than anyone else.

"It's terrible what happened, but yes, it will most definitely mean an uptick of business for Danforth Realty. Evan Weezer always worked as a one man show. He never trained anyone else to take over in case something happened to him. It leaves his business without an experienced salesperson."

It seemed I had a willing interviewee. "Do you mind if I ask you a few questions about the relationship between Mr. Danforth and

Mr. Weezer? I was assigned to write an article about the play, but I find myself without a topic this morning. I thought it would be nice to find out a little more about Evan Weezer. You know, make it more like an obituary about one of the area's top business people."

Roger pursed his mouth and wrinkled his forehead at the phrase top business people. He fidgeted with the stapler on his desk. "I'm not sure I should. He was a competing agent."

"Well, not technically," I said. My friskier journalistic side was poking up its head this morning. "After all, Weezer was number one. It seems, if there was a competition, Mr. Weezer won."

I'd caused just enough fluster with my comment to make him sit up straight and roll his chair forward. "It can hardly be considered a win if Weezer cheated to get there."

"He cheated? I haven't heard the details. What happened?"

His phone rang. I shrank in disappointment, sure I'd lose him to a phone call, which would in turn give him time to rethink telling me about the *cheating* incident. Roger glanced at the screen, released a grunt of frustration and let it go to voicemail. I was in luck.

Roger sat up and straightened his tie, a green silk holiday tie with tiny candy canes. "Five years ago, Danforth Realty was number one in the state. Danny was on a roll, and he seemed unstoppable. There was a waiting line of clients wanting Danny to sell their homes. Weezer was struggling with his business." He said the name Weezer as if he'd just tasted a bitter grape. "He paid a couple to pose as buyers. They came here to Danforth Realty to be represented by Danny. They looked at a few houses but then tried to claim that Danny was trying to force them into signing a contract for a house they didn't want. The claims were false, of course. Danny works hard, but he's never pushy. Not like Weezer is—was," he corrected and then looked contrite about the mistake. "But Weezer paid these people well. They took it all the way to the

Better Business Bureau and the Board of Real Estate. Danny's license was suspended. It took him a year and a fortune in legal fees before it was reinstated. In the meantime, Weezer snaked in and stole his client list. And understandably, it took a long time for the local townsfolk to trust Danny again."

"Were the people arrested as frauds? Did Weezer ever get in trouble for plotting the scheme?" I asked. I was working hard to take in the details of his story. I hadn't taken out my notepad or phone out of fear that it would bring the conversation to a dead stop.

Roger leaned back and twirled a pen around on his desk to avoid looking me straight in the eye. "Unfortunately, there was no actual proof of Weezer's involvement. The couple moved to the other side of the country and withdrew their complaint just before it went in front of a judge. That's how Danny got his license back. But Weezer was ready to swoop in and take away clients. It had to be him."

My shoulders sank. The end to his story was deflating. It would be impossible to write about the scandal and trickery if there was no proof. But if Danny still firmly believed that Evan had caused him such a terrible year of stress and financial loss, then it was easy to see why he despised Evan. It was a part of his past that would leave a long, deep scar.

Past. The word repeated in my head. Danny portrayed a different ghost in the play, but was he actually the Ghost of Christmas Past for Evan Weezer?

"I should get back to my work." Roger's voice pulled me from my thoughts. "You can wait for Danny if you'd like, but it could be several hours."

"Thank you. I'll try back another time." His phone rang.

"I need to answer this," he said.

"Of course. Thanks for your time."

CHAPTER 22

$\mathcal{T}$he morning hadn't been a complete waste. I'd gotten some fairly juicy details about the relationship or, rather, war between the two real estate agents. It seemed to me that I'd uncovered a possible motive for Evan's death. Revenge. Danny had gone through a severe patch of trouble with his business, and if Evan had been behind it, or even if Danny believed it to be true, then he had a strong motive for murder.

I drove my jeep along Butternut Crest and decided to add to my morning's accomplishments by picking up the brooch Chris had secretly purchased for Mom. The last thing I expected, as I turned into the parking lot, was to see Joanna Fritz, Evan's fiancée, scurrying into Larson's Pawn Shop.

I pulled my knitted cap low over my forehead and pushed my scarf up higher so I could slip inside without her recognizing me from the night before. I didn't want my presence to influence her visit to the pawn shop. I had no idea what had brought her to Larson's shop. It probably had nothing to do with the case, but I preferred a *clean* snooping mission.

My winter cover was meant to help me slip inside unnoticed, but Larson's string of jingle bells on the door had the opposite effect. Larson peered at me over the rim of his glasses. Joanna turned briefly to see who had walked through the door. She quickly returned her focus to the small velvet box sitting on the counter in front of her. She didn't even stop for a second glance after I walked in, so either the hat and scarf had done the trick or she was too preoccupied to care. Her eyes were clear, and there was no sign of crying this morning.

I walked over to the window display that held an array of cuckoo clocks and music boxes. I pretended to look them over, all the while keeping my ear turned toward the conversation at the counter.

"This is an engagement ring," Larson said in surprise.

I inched closer to where they were standing and picked up a clock to examine.

"Yes, but I don't need it anymore. How much do you think it's worth?"

"I'm sorry to hear that," Larson said. He obviously had no idea why she no longer needed it. It was easy enough for him to presume that the engagement had been broken. Just as it would be hard to imagine that someone who'd just lost their betrothed to a vicious murder would make selling off the engagement ring a top priority.

It seemed beyond strange and harsh for her to show up at the pawn shop just twelve hours after Evan's murder. Joanna had been extremely distraught at the scene. Was that an act for the investigators?

"Can you leave it with me for a day or two?" Larson asked. "I have a friend who's a jeweler. She can assess the quality of the diamonds and quote me a fair market value."

"I assure you they are of the highest quality. The ring cost seven thousand dollars, or at least that was what I was told."

As surprised as I was to discover that tightfisted Evan Weezer spent that much on a ring, I was equally *not* surprised to learn that he'd actually told his fiancée how much he spent.

"I'm sure it's valuable. I just don't like to make an offer on jewelry without an expert's opinion." Larson was standing firm on his plan.

"Fine. I'll need some kind of receipt that you have it. Will you know by tomorrow morning? I'm in need of the money."

"Yes, tomorrow morning." Larson walked over to his register and pulled out a receipt book.

I felt a sudden pang of guilt when something I hadn't considered popped into my head. It was entirely possible that Joanna needed a large chunk of money to pay for Evan's funeral. Maybe the ring was the only thing of value she owned, and now she had to sell off the one tangible memory of her engagement to pay for her betrothed's burial.

I stayed busy with the glass trinkets on the shelf while Larson wrote up a receipt for the ring. Joanna's fast footsteps clipped across the floor. The jingle bells clanged to signal her exit.

"Can I help you with something?" Larson called from the counter.

"Yes, thank you. I'm here to pick up a brooch. My mother was in here yesterday and she fell in love with an amber brooch. When she wasn't looking, her friend, Chris, purchased it for her. He said he didn't have a chance to sneak it into his pocket before they left. I'm here to pick it up for him."

"Of course. I have it in the back. I found a box for it too."

"Great."

Larson went to the back of the store. Standing in front of the glass cases that held the most valuable items, including antique guns, I was transported back to my first article and coincidentally enough, my first murder investigation. A valuable gun had been lifted from the glass cabinet by the boyfriend of Larson's daughter.

I'd spent time pretending to be interested in the pawned items on the shelves that day too in order to snoop. That case was how I met Jackson. At the time, I never would have guessed that the two of us might see each other socially. Although, last night ended up being more official business than social. I sure hoped that wasn't going to become a pattern when the two of us stepped out together.

Larson returned with the box and brooch. Mom was right. The amber sunflower petals were close in color to Jackson's eyes. "It's beautiful. My mom will be thrilled."

Larson put it in a bag with the receipt.

"I guess that happens more than people imagine," I said, hoping to squeeze a little information out of a man who probably dealt with the occasional engagement ring sale.

"What's that?"

I motioned toward the velvet box sitting near his register.

"Oh, the ring? Not too often. When it's the bride-to-be looking to pawn the ring, it means the groom broke it off or did something despicable enough to make her want to get rid of it just to wash away the heartbreak. And to make sure he doesn't ask for it back. Not sure about this woman though. She seemed less angry than most of them. Usually they're willing to take any offer just to be rid of the thing and to make sure the guy doesn't put it on another woman's finger."

"That all makes sense." While I knew the reason the engagement was off, I didn't feel it was my place to tell Larson. Joanna might have left off that striking detail on purpose.

I picked up the bag with the brooch. "Thank you. Happy holidays."

"You too."

I walked out into the parking lot and the blast of fresh air pushed a new thought into my head. What if the engagement had been broken before Evan's death? Maybe Joanna was easily parting with the ring because her heart had been broken just like Larson mentioned.

I pulled out my phone. It was a stretch but I figured it couldn't hurt. Lana answered on the first ring. "I was just about to call you." She lowered her voice. "Chris is wondering if you can pick up the brooch for Mom. I've got a client coming this morning, so I won't have time."

"Already picked it up."

"Perfect. I'll let Chris know." She was about to hang up.

"Uh, hello, I called you, remember? And it wasn't about the brooch. Just curious, what was the name on the account for the cancelled wedding reception?"

"Hmm, hang on. I've got a ton of names swirling in my head. That was kind of a weird one too because I never met the groom. The entire account was under the bride's name. Poor thing was trying to pay for it herself because her family didn't have the money. Wait a second, it's in my phone." There was a pause, then Lana returned. "The bride was Joanna Fritz."

"Thought it might be. She was supposed to marry the man who was murdered on stage last night."

"Dead Ebenezer was her fiancé? You're kidding."

"Nope and I just saw her in the pawn shop trying to sell the ring to Dick Larson. It was a nice one too. She came to the scene last night, visibly and rightfully shaken. The fact that he had broken off the engagement never came up. Hmm, I guess, as they say, the plot thickens."

"And you worried about writing a boring story. Hey, Mom, Emily and I are going to bake gingerbread cookies tonight at my house if you can pull yourself away from your *investigation*," she teased.

"Well, I'm certainly not letting a cookie baking session take place without me. I'll see you later."

A text came through from Jackson just as I climbed into the car.

"Lunch at Layers at noon? I want to make up for last night's disastrous date."

I stared at the word date and rubbed my finger over it. It was real and not just a typo. I was fairly certain it was a date but now I had proof. "I would like that. And I've found out a few details that might interest you."

"Great. See you then."

CHAPTER 23

*J*ackson was outside of Layers, talking on his phone, as I walked up. He hung up and put his phone in the pocket of his blue windbreaker. His smile warmed me inside, much like a hot cup of cocoa.

"Hey, Bluebird, busy morning?" He held open the door for me and we walked inside. As always seemed to be the case when I stepped into a place with Detective Jackson, a number of curious glances and outright stares fell our direction. I wondered if it was just because he was a member of law enforcement. Or maybe they'd seen him walk into places with so many different women, people were just getting a gander of his newest friend. That notion soured my empty stomach some so I pushed it away. I was hungry, and I'd been thinking about the Danny Kaye, cream cheese, tomato and basil on a toasted whole grain bun ever since Jackson suggested Layers.

"I have been busy," I said as we slid into a booth at the back. Jackson offered me a menu. "I already know what I want. I found out early on that if I didn't walk in here with my mind made up, I risked spending my entire lunch break deciding."

He chuckled. "There are a lot of choices, however, I usually trade off between Boris Karloff and Jack Benny. It's Karloff's turn today." He stuck the menus back into their holder.

Mitch, the server, a young guy the owner, Ballard, hired for the holiday season and who she quickly made permanent, came to the table to take our order. He returned right away with my hot tea and Jackson's soda.

"Anything new with the case?" I asked as I squeezed lemon into my tea.

"He definitely died from the stab wound."

"Pretty much figured that one out already. Come on, don't keep a nosy journalist hanging. There must be something else."

"I'm sure there is. My problem is that because we're short-handed I'm working on so many cases, I hardly have time to focus on anything. I've got someone researching Weezer's business history and potentially unhappy clients. Sometimes it's easier to look for a motive and hope it leads to a suspect."

"Well then, I might have something for you." I primly placed my napkin on my lap. "Since I am writing an article about the play—"

"You mean the ten minute production of *A Christmas Carol* with a grisly new twist?"

"Yes, obviously the focus of my article has shifted. But since it's part of my assignment, I decided to interview Danny Danforth and get a few more insights to Evan's character and their abrasive relationship."

Jackson took a drink of his cola. "I hope you got a confession out of him. Then I could check one off of the list."

"Not exactly. In fact, I didn't even get to see Danny. Turns out he's very busy now that his biggest competitor is dead."

Jackson sensed immediately what I was getting at. He tilted his head side to side. "Could definitely be classified as a motive. Money is always a powerful incentive."

"Couple that with revenge, and you've got a double whammy."

"A double whammy, eh?" Jackson leaned back and gazed at me with those amber jewel eyes. It threw me off my train of thought for a second.

I gathered myself. "A few years back, Danny was taken to court by a disgruntled couple who claimed he was forcing them into a bad contract. He had to pay big legal fees and even lost his real estate license and, therefore, his income for nearly a year. He'd held the number one agent position before that, but his reputation was destroyed. Eventually, the couple dropped the suit. While Danny was on suspension, Evan Weezer zipped his way right up to the top spot. Danny is convinced he paid the couple to cause the ruckus and ruin his business."

"Did Danny ever prove it?"

"No, but he still believes it. That would leave a nasty sting if your business was ruined by a competitor who was playing dirty tricks." I sat back with a satisfied smile. "There you have it—the double whammy. Revenge and money."

Jackson nodded. "Good work. We'll have to dig deeper into that scandal and see what we find."

Mitch delivered our food.

I grabbed the salt and pepper. "Danny Danforth might not have been the only one with a motive. I found something out about another person during my morning adventures."

Jackson poured ketchup on his fries. "Sounds like you had a way more productive morning than me. Is this someone from the cast or crew of the play?"

"No but she was there last night, and she had a good reason to be there."

"The fiancée." He said confidently. I'd learned early on that Jackson was always one step ahead of me in my own thoughts.

"Yes, only she was not his fiancée last night."

His brow arched in confusion.

"Ah ha, I finally stayed ahead of you." I cheered lightly. "You always seem to know exactly what I'm going to say, and frankly, it's pretty darn annoying."

He shrugged. "It's a gift. If I didn't have it, I'd probably be shifting boxes around the evidence room or mopping up stuff on the morgue floor." He stared down at his Boris Karloff, a burger with guacamole and grilled onions. "Probably could have left that last part about the morgue off. So why wasn't she a fiancée last night?" he asked as he lifted the burger with both hands and took a good, manly bite.

"My sister, Lana, got word on Tuesday that one of her January wedding receptions had been canceled because the groom broke it off. Lana said the woman was out a hefty deposit because of how late it was. My sister had already spent money on decorations and linens."

"The jilted bride was Joanna Fritz?" Jackson wiped his mouth after I pointed out a tiny drip of guacamole.

"Yes, and Joanna didn't waste any time trying to cash in the engagement ring. Probably to help replace the money she lost on the reception deposit and, no doubt, dress and photographer deposit. There are so many expenses that come with a wedding. Lana said the groom apparently had no hand and little interest in the wedding. It was all on Joanna's shoulders, and she was paying for everything herself."

"That Weezer really was a Scrooge." Jackson's phone buzzed as he lifted his cola. "It'll be short. It's the precinct."

I took a few minutes to enjoy my Danny Kaye while Jackson answered a quick call. He was plunging his straw up and down in the glass with his free hand.

"Straw," I blurted just loud enough to catch his attention.

"I'll head out there as soon as I'm done eating," Jackson said to whoever was on the other side. He hung up. "Did you want me to ask Mitch for a straw?"

"No, I didn't mean that kind of straw. I was so tired by the end of the night, I nearly forgot the two things I found when I searched the perimeter of the tent." I picked up my coat that was lying next to me on the seat and fished through the pockets. I pulled out the tissue wrapped candy package and the tissue wrapped piece of straw.

Jackson sat forward with interest. Suddenly I wished I had something a little more exciting to show him. "This is just a candy wrapper. I'm sure it got swept in from the festival, but I found this too." I held the tissue on my hand and opened it to reveal the single strand of straw."

Jackson stared at it for a moment. "That looks like straw."

"It is straw. I found it under the border of the tent right next to the place where Evan was stabbed. I know it doesn't look like much, but when I searched around the tent area, there wasn't any logical place it could have come from."

"It was windy last night. Straw is light. It could have come from fifty miles away on a farm." Jackson returned his attention to his burger.

I was somewhat disappointed at his lack of interest, even if I could have predicted it. It wasn't as if I presented him with some major piece of evidence. Just a slim piece of straw that, as he pointed out, could have traveled miles on the wind. Or it could have traveled several blocks from the Nativity manger.

"I know it's not much but maybe I should toss this nugget out. The piece of straw might not have traveled to the tent on the wind at all. What if someone brought it there on their clothes?"

He peered at me over his burger as he continued chewing, waiting me for to fill in something interesting.

"Joanna Fritz, the broken-hearted bride-to-be, is in charge of the festival's Nativity scene."

"Yep, she mentioned that last night." He wiped his hands. "So you think she dragged that piece of straw on her clothing, and it fell off during the time she waited in the dark to stab her ex-fiancé?"

"Yes," I said confidently. "It's just one theory, of course, but I think it's a good one. And there is both passion and money in that motive. Another double whammy."

Jackson nodded. "Better than anything we've got so far. I'll keep Joanna Fritz on my radar. When my radar's in town. I've got to head out to Smithville for another case I'm wrapping up."

He was nearly finished with his burger. I handed him half of my Danny Kaye and got to work on my portion. This time, I was the one with something on my lip. But instead of pointing it out, Jackson reached right over and wiped the cream cheese off with his thumb. I should have felt a bit embarrassed, but I was too busy catching my breath from the surprise gesture.

I finished what I could of my lunch. I needed to save room for gingerbread cookies. Jackson paid for the lunch, and we walked out to just as many stares as when we walked in.

"Then our *Christmas Carol* plot thickens," I said as we stepped into the cold air.

"How's that?"

"I've found a Ghost of Christmas Past. Danny Danforth and the problems Evan caused him years ago. Our Ghost of Christmas Yet to Be could be Joanna Fritz. They were supposed to be married in January and she was looking forward to a bright future as she mentioned more than once."

"Who is the Ghost of Christmas Present?" he asked.

"I have someone lined up for that part. I'm heading over to Evan's realty office to talk to his assistant, Tim, father of Timmy Junior, on the crutches. I need more information for my article or it will only be a paragraph long."

"Just don't do anything dangerous," he said.

"Not my style. I'm far too sneaky for that."

He walked me to my jeep. We stopped next to it. His thick hair fluttered in the breeze, and the afternoon winter sun made his eyes glittery gold.

His mouth turned up in a crooked grin. "You know, Bluebird, there's one big flaw with your *Christmas Carol* plot."

"What's that?"

"Ebenezer Scrooge didn't end up with a tent stake in his back."

CHAPTER 24

A local television news van was just pulling away from Weezer Realty as I parked the jeep. It looked as if my timing couldn't have been more perfect. It seemed I'd arrived after the flurry of activity. With Weezer being a well-known businessman in the area and with his death being so terribly public, it was no surprise to see the news crews.

It was also not surprising to see that the office was basically deserted. Tim Barton was sitting behind a partition talking on his phone when I walked inside.

The differences between the Danforth and Weezer realty offices were stark, to say the least. Danforth Realty was a small, unassuming office space with the traditional big box store kind of furniture, pressed board desks, slightly uncomfortable chairs and cheap art on the walls. Weezer's office was sleek with polished wood, glass partitions and flat screen computers on every desk. I could easily imagine it as a bustling work place with clients flowing in and out and the large white board with listings and recent sales moving as fluidly as the fish inside the massive fish tank glowing from the back wall.

I stood at the reception desk, even though there was no one behind it and waited until Tim finished his phone call. It would have been nice to get a few employee's comments for the article, but Tim was the person who interested me the most. I wasn't sure where Jackson stood on Tim, but I had not marked him off of my own person of interest list. I'd witnessed firsthand how badly Evan treated his assistant.

Tim was keenly aware of my presence, but he continued his phone call. He seemed to be perusing several home listings as he spoke to the person on the other side, leading me to believe that it was a client. Weezer was dead but other people's lives went on. People needed places to live, after all.

One wall of the building was covered with awards and framed articles about Weezer's rise to the top. Photos of staff members and clients standing in front of new houses took up a third of the wall. I moved closer to check out a picture of Evan. He looked considerably younger, and he was standing next to another man, about the same age. They were each standing on the side of a large for sale sign on a vast empty lot. The lot was surrounded by apartments and office buildings. A big red SOLD sticker was pasted across the front of the sign.

"We're technically closed for business." Tim's voice pulled me from my photo survey. "I don't know if you've heard—" He stopped when I turned to him. "Oh, you're the reporter from *Junction Times*." There was no derision in his tone, but it wasn't exactly welcoming either. He reached me and glanced at the picture that had drawn my interest. "That's Evan with his late partner, John Marlin."

Evan Weezer had a late partner with the last name Marlin. I realized it would be totally inappropriate to chirp in excitement at yet another similarity to *A Christmas Carol* so I kept a lid on it and smiled politely. "Late partner? So Mr. Marlin is—"

"Dead, yes. I never knew the man. He died eight or nine years ago. I was just about to get a bottle of water from the lounge, can I interest you in one?"

"No, thanks. I just had lunch, so I'm good."

He disappeared through a door and returned with a bottle of water. Tim was not the same man I saw hunched over, nervous and nearly groveling in front of his boss. His thin shoulders stood much higher and straighter. His manner seemed relaxed as if a heavy burden had been lifted from his life. Which was probably not far from the truth.

His grip was firm and steady as he twisted off the bottle cap. "I've already given an interview to the press. In fact, a local station just left with their crew."

"Yes, I saw the van pulling away. I was originally assigned to cover the play for the paper, but that is no longer going to happen. I thought I could write up a little something about the future of Weezer Realty. Since it was number one in the state, I imagine people around here are going to miss it if it shuts down. Or will someone else take the helm? Did Weezer have someone in mind to take over if something happened to him?"

"I don't think Evan considered himself mortal like the rest of us. I don't know for certain, but I don't believe he made any kind of will or trust. He had no close family. A man like him rarely does."

I followed Tim to his cubicle. He was kind enough to roll over the chair from the neighboring desk. "Naturally everyone took the day off today. There is still plenty of outstanding paperwork to do, but it seemed like a good idea to close up shop today. I made the decision." He shifted higher in his seat, seemingly pleased with his new role as decision maker.

"I think that was a good call. Although, you didn't give yourself a day off," I noted.

"There were calls to be made. Even knowing he was performing in the play last night, Evan still had a full calendar today. I needed to let those people know the appointments were cancelled. Of course, most of them had already heard the news, but I thought calling them was the polite thing to do."

"It's just good business." I rolled the chair a little closer. "Evan didn't have any close relatives to leave the business to? What about friends?"

"Evan liked to joke that he had no need for friends, just acquaintances with big pockets. He had a fiancée. We were all shocked, here in the office, that some poor woman would subject herself to a life with Evan Weezer but then for some people being rich is worth the sacrifice. Except, I think something had happened between Evan and Joanna. When I asked him about the wedding invitations being mailed, he told me not to hold my breath. I figured he'd either taken me off the guest list or cancelled the wedding altogether. I decided it was the latter because his side of the list was going to be short anyhow."

I decided not to impart any of the details I knew about the engagement. "What will happen to this real estate office since Evan didn't plan for his death?"

"I suppose it will be closed down or sold. I'm not entirely sure, but I know some of the office personnel are spending their day off looking for new jobs. Most of them were just part-time people anyhow. For all the money he made, Evan was pretty stingy when it came to paying his staff. Me included."

"What will you do now? I suppose this has been a big blow for you."

"It will force me to do something I've been meaning to do for a long time. I'm going to finish my real estate license classes so I can sell houses on my own. I've learned a lot about the business working for Evan, indirectly more than directly," he added. "He wasn't much of a teacher. Most of the time he was miserable and impatient, always quick to point out my mistakes, while, at the same time, never saying thanks or good job." Tim's eye twitched as he rolled off on his short, quiet rant about his former boss. He stopped himself with a drink of water. He rubbed his twitching eye. "Sorry, I sometimes deal with anxiety. Also a result of working for Evan Weezer. Still, I stuck it out, and I'm glad I did."

"Oh, why is that?" I asked. Tim was much freer with his personal insight than I expected. It was giving me a good clear look at their relationship. I could easily conclude that Tim was not going to suffer much from the loss of his boss, with the exception of having to find a new job.

Tim seemed hesitant to answer my question at first. He moved a few papers unnecessarily around his desk for a second, then sat back. "I've been the one keeping the database going for the business. It's a large database. Once I have my license, I'll have access to contact information for many potential clients."

I was slightly disappointed at his response. I wasn't exactly sure what I was waiting for, but a database of potential customers wasn't it. "I'm sure that will come in handy when you're just starting out." It wasn't anything earth shattering, but it was plain to see that Tim was going to recover from the shock of the murder just fine. Maybe too fine.

I sat forward and admired the family picture on his desk. Timmy Junior was not on crutches in the picture taken by a lake. He was holding a soccer ball under his arm and grinning impishly as he held up bunny ears behind his dad's head.

"How is your son doing?" I asked.

He looked surprised at the question.

"I was in the tent the day he hurt his ankle. I know it took some convincing for Evan to let you leave to be with him in the emergency room."

His cheeks reddened some at the comment as if he was ashamed that I'd witnessed him beg and plead with his boss. "He's fine, thanks. Evan could be a real bear when it came to time off. He never had kids, so he couldn't understand what I was going through." He was making excuses. I wondered if he was being cautious not to let on how he really felt about Evan's management style.

"I have to say, my only children are two spoiled dogs, but I could sense your distress when it seemed Evan might not let you leave."

"I knew he'd eventually give in. Look, in most respects, he was an awful man. I hate talking like this so soon after his death, but Evan was not nice. He was rich and greedy and thought only of himself. I wish I could feel some sadness at his loss, but that just hasn't happened. Once the shock wore off, the only thing I felt was —I hate to admit it, but I felt relief. That makes me sound like a monster, I know."

"No, I don't think that at all. I think you were a brave, patient man to put up with him. I know it was for your family and your future in the business, but not many people would have stuck it out with a man like Evan Weezer." My imaginative mind went straight to casting Tim in a dual role, not just as Bob Cratchit but as the Ghost of Christmas Present. The three spirits were there to bring some conscience and compassion to a miserly man, who lacked all good qualities. I was sure somewhere throughout their relationship, Evan must have witnessed enough decency through his assistant to at least give him pause about his own behavior. Or maybe I just wanted to fill in all the parts of the story.

Tim seemed to enjoy the compliments I paid him. I hoped he was open to a few more prying questions. I decided to toss them out there anyway.

"Tim, since you spent so much time with Evan, do you have any idea at all who might have killed him?"

I worried he might be taken aback by my question. Instead, he was ready with a few answers, including the one I expected. "Evan crossed so many people in business, there are almost too many to consider. But the one that stands out the most is Danny Danforth." He put up his hands. "Not that I'm accusing him, but his career was ruined by Evan. He's growing back his business now. Evan's death will definitely help."

"What about other people here in this office?" I asked, realizing that there might be an entire pool of employees we hadn't even considered. "Were any of them at the play last night?"

"Here? No, I was the only office person at the play. Most of them are just part-timers, people who run errands and sit for open houses. And Evan couldn't be bothered with handling his employees. I was the middleman. That spared them from having to deal with Evan directly. Most of them had little interaction with Evan. Most mornings, he would walk straight through that door with his phone already tucked between his shoulder and ear. He'd toss mail, contracts and paperwork onto my desk without a hello to anyone. Not even me."

I shook my head. "He obviously never took any courses in leadership or management."

"If he did, he decided to do the exact opposite of everything he learned." Tim laughed weakly.

"I won't take up any more of your time." I stood up. "I hope you're able to move on with your career in realty."

"Thanks," he said as he walked me to the door. He waved and locked the door behind me. His life had changed dramatically with Evan's death, but did he despise the man enough to kill him?

CHAPTER 25

I finished putting my hair up in a ponytail, a proper hairstyle for gingerbread baking.

"What is it with that man showing up at all hours, on any day and for seemingly no occasion at all," Edward griped from the kitchen.

I leaned out of the bathroom. "What man?" I asked.

"The brute with the wild hair and wolfish eyes."

The comb slipped right out of my fingers. I stooped down to pick it up and managed to smack my shoulder on the vanity on the way up. "Ouch, darn, darn." I rubbed it as I hurried out of the bathroom.

"How is it possible to injure oneself while combing hair?" Edward asked.

"Oh shush and disappear too. I wasn't expecting him."

"Exactly my point. Terrible manners."

I rolled my shoulder to ease the pain. Redford and Newman were already at the door, waiting to greet Jackson. The night air was fiercely cold as I opened the door. Jackson was wearing a black hooded jacket and a black scarf covered part of his chin.

"If I didn't recognize those amber eyes, I might very well have just slammed the door in your face and ran to hide under my bed." I motioned him inside, which took him longer because Redford and Newman would not let him pass without a few hearty pats.

He reached up and pushed the hood off and hooked his fingers around the edge of the scarf to pull it free from his face. "I guess I didn't get a good look at myself in the rearview mirror when I parked. It might explain why the woman at the walk up burger window gasped and backed away from the register when I went to order my burger.

"You ate another hamburger?" I asked. "Seems like I just watched you vacuum down a Boris Karloff not six hours ago."

"I tend to revert back to my terrible teenage junk food years when I'm mired down in work."

"Did you get any further on the case today?" I asked.

"Nope, I've got three other cases going at the same time, including a bank robbery in Smithville. I've got my team working on a few things though. Unfortunately, my team is still pretty new at this. I'm short skilled help right now." He smiled at me. "With the exception of one highly curious and skilled reporter. I like the ponytail. Highlights your beautiful eyes."

A sound that could only be interpreted as a haughty Englishman's scoff shot down the hallway from the kitchen. My heart stopped for a full ten seconds while I waited, frozen with fear that Jackson had heard it. I released a long, silent breath when he asked about the rest of my day.

"I went to Weezer Realty after lunch," I began, but was stopped by my phone buzzing. I pulled it out of my pocket.

"Gingerbread men wait for no one," Lana texted.

"It's my sister. We're making gingerbread cookies tonight."

"Wow, can't remember the last time I made gingerbread cookies," he said.

My laugh echoed off the entry, but I stopped when I realized he wasn't kidding. "Wait, you baked cookies?"

"With my mom and sisters. I was more the taste tester than the baker, but I got my hands in the flour some," he said proudly.

"That is so cute. Did you wear an apron?"

"Nope, I drew a line at the apron."

"Why don't you come with me and bake some cookies? With any luck, my mom will be too busy cutting gingerbread men to embarrass me with childhood stories." I quickly worried that he'd say no, and I'd feel silly for asking. His hesitation felt like a weight on my chest. Why on earth had I invited him?

"If you're sure your family won't mind."

I was elated but instantly wondering if I'd lost my mind. This wouldn't just be a chance meeting out on the sidewalk during a busy festival. It would be Jackson trapped in a kitchen with my sisters and Mom and any embarrassing question or narrative they felt like bringing up just to see me squirm.

"Great," I said and was keenly aware of the forced enthusiasm. Fortunately, just like Edward's big scoff, Jackson didn't notice. "Let me just make sure the dogs' water bowl is filled. I'll be right back." I rudely left my guest in the entry and dashed to the kitchen. The water bowl inspection was a ruse that would give me just enough time alone to send Emily a warning text. I knew if anyone would be kind and help out a now terrified sister, it would be Emily.

"I'm on my way and I'm bringing Jackson so tell Mom and Lana nothing embarrassing or I'm taking back their gifts."

Emily sent back the smiley face and thumbs-up emojis. I knew she was the perfect point person at a critical time like this.

I returned to the entry where Jackson was petting the dogs. No ghost in sight. I'd left him alone in such a hurry, I hadn't even considered the frightening possibility of Edward showing up to play a trick or make a nuisance of himself. He was especially good at sending Newman's tennis ball sailing through the house with no particular starting point. And it was always up to me to convince my guests that the house was on a slight tilt or that Newman knew how to throw his own ball.

I was a mix of excitement, nerves and pure terror. Jackson's easy going smile helped calm my frayed edges. He patted Redford one last time and opened the front door.

"All right, let's go eat some gingerbread," I said cheerily.

CHAPTER 26

*C*innamon, cloves and the rich, deep scent of molasses permeated every inch of Lana's vast kitchen. Her long maple work table was dusted with flour and scraps of gingerbread dough. Plump ginger people lined one side of the table waiting for their turn in the oven. Jackson, Mom and I had settled at Lana's white porcelain kitchen table to squeeze creamy glaze in the shape of buttons and bows. Jackson was far better at nibbling off arms and legs than adding in details.

Just like his easy going smile had calmed my nerves back at the inn, his laid back, confident manner also quickly wiped away the first few moments of awkwardness and overly polite greetings when we walked into Lana's house.

Emily was rolling out the last ball of dough, and Lana was standing ready at the oven, waiting for the next batch to be done. This was going to be a crunchy batch. Lana and I liked the crispy gingerbread. While Emily and Mom preferred theirs just a tad under-baked so they stayed soft and chewy. I quickly discovered that Jackson was not picky and gladly ate either kind of cookie.

"Just how did you two meet?" Mom pointedly referred her sudden question to Jackson.

Jackson put down the cookie he'd been nibbling, sat back and favored me with a teasing gaze. "I was called in to investigate a murder scene at a park in a nearby town. Let's just say there was a highly curious and tenacious journalist at the site."

"Tenacious," Lana laughed. "Perfect word choice."

I tossed a few red sprinkles at her. "I'm sure I could come up with some perfect word choices for you too."

Lana brushed a red sprinkle off her shoulder. "I should hope so. You *are* a journalist after all."

"Quiet, you two," Mom said and turned her gleaming smile back to Jackson. "Go on," she prodded.

"Believe it or not, our first real conversation happened while I was standing in the park, and Sunni was perched up in a tree over-looking the scene."

"Sunni," Mom said with feigned shock. She knew darn well that I wouldn't have given a second thought to climbing a tree to get a news scoop, but it seemed she wanted to pretend she raised much more of a lady. "You could have been hurt. You're not a little girl in blue jeans and sneakers anymore."

I laughed. "Did you think I climbed the tree in a dress? I still wear blue jeans and sneakers every chance I get, by the way." I turned to Jackson. "And to think I was mortified that my mom or sisters would come up with some embarrassing tale about my childhood, when, all the while, my guest had the story to tell."

Jackson shrugged. "She asked. It's not as if I had to embellish it." He bit the head off the cookie he was holding. "I think I'm leaning toward the crispy now. But I'll probably change my mind with the next batch of soft and chewy."

Nick and Chris walked into the kitchen with the quart of milk they'd taken a good hour to buy. "Where did you go for the milk?" Emily asked. "Wisconsin?"

"We got sidetracked," Nick said. "The ice cream store was giving away free samples of pumpkin spice ice cream."

Emily wiped the flour from her hands. "Yum, did you bring some for the rest of us?"

Both men fell sheepishly quiet as they exchanged 'oops' glances with each other. It seemed Nick and Chris were becoming fast friends, which I'm sure made my mom happy. Of course, everyone got along well with Nick. He was always pleasant and generous and humble. He was the exact opposite of Evan Weezer. That thought reminded me of my visit to Weezer Realty.

I finished the bow tie on the last gingerbread man and dropped my pastry bag into the bowl. "I think I could use a little break from the heady scent of clove and ginger." I motioned toward the door as I looked at Jackson. "Care to join me on the front porch, or will you find it too hard to drag yourself away from warm cookies?"

Jackson wiped his hands on his napkin. "Actually, that's a good idea. I think I need some gingerbread intervention."

Mom burst into an exaggerated laugh at his quip. She had been shining with sparkly school girl winks and smiles all night. It was kind of fun to watch.

I pulled my coat tightly shut as we stepped onto Lana's porch and sat on her swing. It was a clear, crisp night. The sky looked as if someone had thrown a net of diamonds over black slate.

"I love this kind of weather," I said as Jackson pushed with his long legs, sending the swing rocking back and forth.

"I do too. Snow's been pretty light this year too, which makes the whole winter thing a little easier. I like your family. I hardly ever see mine. Everyone is kind of spread out, so this was nice. Think I ate ten holiday's worth of gingerbread tonight."

"You were munching those poor, unsuspecting guys down pretty fast. Reminded me of my brother, Neal. He used to eat the cookies faster than Mom could lift them to the cooling rack."

"I didn't know you had a brother," Jackson said. "Guess there are a lot of things we still don't know about each other."

I swung my feet back and forth as the swing rocked. "I'm not all that big of a mystery. You pretty much get what you see."

Jackson put his arm around my shoulder. "That suits me just fine."

Emotion and a slight case of the jitters swirled through me. Don't get hooked yet, Sunni, I told myself. As much as you *weren't* a mystery, the tall handsome guy next to you was certainly a big one.

"I invited you out here to tell you a few things I found out today at Weezer Realty."

"Darn, I was hoping you asked me out here for that first kiss."

"Hmm, with my mom and sisters right inside? It's still not the right kaboom moment."

"Point taken," he said. "What did you find out?"

"Tim is not the slightest bit distraught about Evan's death. In fact, I think he was feeling pretty good today. He even made an executive decision to give everyone the day off. He's got plans to get his real estate license, and he has Evan's database on his computer to give him a big stepping stone into the business."

Jackson reached up with his free hand and combed his fingers back through his hair, providing me with a nice view of his perfectly chiseled profile. He was waiting for me to continue, but that was all I had.

"I guess that might not have been worth pulling you away from the gingerbread, eh?" I asked.

"I spoke to Tim last night, and he admitted that he wasn't sad. I think he felt somewhat guilty about it, but he was being honest. I didn't get the sense that he was a killer but then I didn't spend too much time with him. He does have a motive, not a strong one but it's there. Sounded like Weezer was a really awful guy to work for."

I was feeling somewhat deflated. "Then I guess there's not

much else to say about my visit. However, I did add another significant cast member to my more macabre version of *A Christmas Carol*. Turns out Evan Weezer had a late partner, and I don't mean the tardy kind. He's dead, a goner, just like the story." I turned slightly toward him. "And here's the kicker—his name is—"

"John Marlin," Jackson finished for me.

I blew a puff of air from my mouth that left behind a white cloud. "You really know how to take the steam out of someone's kettle."

"Sorry. We've been looking into his past for possible suspects. My team came upon John Marlin's name as Weezer's partner." He titled his head toward me. "Deceased, or as you put it, a goner." He took my hand in his. His slightly callused fingers were warm as they wrapped around mine. "If it's any consolation, when I got the report about the partner, I immediately thought about you and your *Christmas Carol* comparison."

"That does help," I admitted. "Just out of curiosity, was that the only time you thought of me today?" My cheeks warmed at my own brazen question. It had popped out before I could rethink it.

He squeezed my hand tighter and gazed at me so intently, I felt the warmth of his hand all the way up my arm. "You know it's not, Bluebird" he said quietly.

The front door burst open. Lana's laughter broke the heat that had filled the air between us. Our gazes pulled reluctantly apart.

"You've got to come back inside, Jackson. Mom's about to tell Chris the Christmas story when a four-year-old Sunni snuck downstairs in the middle of the night and opened everyone's gifts and stockings."

"*Must* she," I complained.

"Think I'm going to need to listen in on that." Jackson got up and offered me his hand.

"*Must* you," I complained.

I trudged to the door. "It was Mom's fault. She sat me down in front of the television to watch *The Grinch* that night. I was sure he was going to come in and take the gifts before we had a chance to open them." I smiled back at Jackson as we walked inside. "That's my alibi, and I'm sticking to it."

CHAPTER 27

*J*ackson had so much work and on top of that he was going to be spending a good portion of his day in court testifying in another case. There were other people working on the murder case, but I decided it was my *civic duty* as a journalist to continue looking into Evan Weezer's death.

I decided to return to the scene of the crime. The festival was still going strong despite the catastrophic end to the play. The sky was clear above, making the air below nearly brittle with cold. I decided a mid morning cup of hot apple cider was just what I needed before exploring the crime scene. I pulled my gloves off and shoved them into my pocket to warm them around the cup. I stood sipping the cider, watching the horse and carriage team go past. Aurora, a woman I knew only because of her unusual name, was dressed in plush green velvet livery with a matching top hat. The two horses were thick with their winter coats and adorned with tiny silver bells. Red ribbons had been braided through their black manes. A young couple sat in the carriage snapping selfies with their cameras. Apparently, the experience was less about the charming, old-fashioned ride through town and more about getting a good shot for Instagram.

With cider grasped tightly in my hand, I headed down the block and around the corner toward the theater tent. I stopped abruptly in disappointment, splashing a few drops of hot cider on my thumb. A team of four people had just finished loading the folded tent onto the back of a large truck. The only things remaining at the site were a few pieces of leftover trash and the trailer Evan Weezer had brought in for his personal use. The yellow caution tape had been removed from around the steps, which meant the police were done with their forensics search.

As I got closer, I noticed the trailer door was ajar. Someone was inside, possibly the person in charge of hauling it away. I was just in time. I tried to come up with a good excuse for searching inside the trailer, but my mind was drawing a blank. When in a pickle, I always resorted to pulling out my press pass.

I walked up the steps, and the sudden notion that I might be about to surprise the murderer returning to the scene dashed through my head. I was relieved to find Scottie inside stuffing Evan's Scrooge frock coat into a plastic garment bag.

Her eyes rounded and she pressed her hand to her throat. "Sunni, you scared me. I didn't expect anyone to come up those steps." She giggled. "It's silly but for a second I worried that the murderer had returned to the scene."

I smiled. "Then you and I think alike. When I heard someone shuffling around in here, I thought the same thing."

"But that didn't stop you from walking in." She shook her head. "I've got to say, you journalists sure are gutsy when it comes to getting your story. Unfortunately, it's just me. I needed to pick up Evan's costumes. They belong to the theater department at the city college." She took hold of the zipper pull on the garment bag while holding the hanger with the other hand. Like most zippers, it was stubborn.

"Here, let me help you with that." I stepped forward.

Scottie released the zipper. "I'll hold the hanger if you wouldn't mind zipping it shut."

"Absolutely." Just as I lifted my hand to the zipper, I noticed something on the lapel of the frock coat. It was a wiry brown strand of fake hair. I pulled it free and shut the zipper. I held the fiber up to the light coming through the small window.

"What do you have there?" Scottie squinted at it. "That looks like hair from a fake beard or wig," she noted, confirming my first guess.

"I don't recall—" I said, only I did recall perfectly. "Was Evan wearing a brown wig or a beard with his costume?"

"No. There were a few wigs in the costume collection but none of them brown. That looks like a strand of hair from Danny's fake beard." Again, Scottie settled my hunch.

"I wonder how Danny's beard hair got on Evan's frock coat." I tossed it out there, hoping Scottie might have some insight. It was entirely possible the strand was blown loose, and it just happened to adhere to the lapel of the coat.

"It does seem strange considering the two men always made a point of walking a wide berth around each other. That is, when they weren't on stage. Close proximity was unavoidable during rehearsal." Scottie set to work putting the top hat back into its box. She stopped and tapped her chin. "Although, there was a slight, sort of physically combative moment between the two men during dress rehearsal." Her shoulders dropped. "Why, I'd forgotten all about the incident until just now."

"Combative? What happened?"

"Well, combative might be too strong of a term, but Danny and Evan clashed shoulders as they walked past each other on stage. I think it was accidental. The stage was small, and Danny takes up more room than the average person. But rather than apologize to each other, they both glowered at each other for a tense moment before moving on with the rehearsal. Boy, if looks could kill, those two would have dropped right where they stood." She covered her mouth. "That sounded terrible considering Evan did drop where he stood."

"I suppose there's never a right way to talk about a murder victim." I walked over and pulled a tissue out from the box on the shelf of the trailer. I tucked the hair inside of it and pushed it into my pocket. "Do you mind if I snoop around? I won't move anything."

"Go ahead. They'll be hauling away this trailer today. The police took Evan's computer and phone and the clothes he was wearing before he changed into costume. And, of course, the night shirt and cap he was wearing when—Well, you know."

"Yes." I browsed the table and mirror area where Evan must have sat to get ready for the stage. There was a compact of pale foundation and dark charcoal pencils for adding wrinkles and rings under the eyes. Nothing looked out of place. The police had already determined that Evan had been stabbed just outside the tent, so his trailer was not technically part of the murder scene.

Scottie's phone went off with a *Deck the Halls* ringtone. She pulled it out. I perused the rest of the trailer. Nothing stood out as important, but the holiday ringtone spurred another question. In the midst of the chaos, the seconds after Evan collapsed on stage, I'd heard *Jingle Bells* playing on a phone somewhere outside of the tent. I hadn't thought of it again until Scottie's phone rang.

Scottie's phone conversation ended quickly.

"I noticed your festive ringtone," I said as she returned to her task of packing up the costume.

"Yes, my daughter did that to my phone. I didn't even know she changed it until it rang one day. I thought it was someone's radio. Then I realized it was my phone."

"Does it change to other songs or is it just *Deck the Halls?*"

"Just the one song. Although, if she had asked, I would have preferred *Have a Holly Jolly Christmas*. That's my favorite."

"This might seem like an odd question, but do you know if anyone else on the cast and crew had a holiday ringtone? Specifically *Jingle Bells*?"

"Hmm, I think I heard a few holiday ringtones during practices, but I'm not sure I heard *Jingle Bells*. And with all the holiday music blasting through the festival speakers and in the department stores and markets, it's all kind of a blur."

"What about Danny Danforth? Any chance you heard his ringtone?"

"I'm not sure." Her mouth pulled into a grim line. "Is this about the strand of beard on the coat?" Scottie was connecting the dots of my questions.

"No, not at all. I'm just finding out details about that night because I need to write an article about the incident."

Scottie folded up a gray cravat with a look of concern. "I know Danny disliked Evan, but he's really just a big teddy bear. I can't imagine him killing anyone."

"No, of course not, and I agree. He seems like a big teddy bear. Well, I'll get out of your way. Have a good holiday."

"Same to you. I hope you find what you're looking for. And I hope the police find the murderer soon. It's sort of hard to think about celebrating with a killer on the loose."

"Very true. Good-bye, Scottie." I walked out of the trailer with the strand of beard and a new line of thinking. Would a *Jingle Bells* ringtone lead us to Evan's killer?"

CHAPTER 28

*M*yrna had taken an extended lunch break to do some shopping. Parker left early for a meeting with Jerold Newsom, the owner of the paper, and Chase was out for the day. He told Parker he was working from home, but Myrna texted halfway through her shopping trip to say she saw Chase walk into a jewelry store. She was sure he was looking at engagement rings. All I knew was that I had a rare hour to myself in the newsroom.

I pulled a clean sheet of paper out of the printer and decided to sketch out a quick diagram of evidence and possible suspects and motives. The middle circle was easy to fill. Evan Weezer was the victim. He'd been stabbed with a tent stake. Since I happened to be on site when the corner of the tent broke free and whipped wildly around, nearly collapsing the entire structure, I knew who was in the vicinity when the stake was pulled free. It seemed logical to conclude that the corner whipped up soon after the stake was removed, which narrowed down the suspect list. I started enthusiastically with that assumption, only to then theorize that the person who took the stake probably didn't hang around. Which brought me back to square one.

I surrounded the center circle with boxes and wrote in a few names, people who had a heavy connection with Evan. Number one on the list was Danny Danforth. Danny had motive. Evan ruined his career, and his death would help Danny rebuild his business. Black paint and shoe prints put Danny close to the stage entrance where Evan took his last few steps. It didn't match up with the blood evidence that showed Evan was stabbed outside of the tent. A fiber of beard from Danny's costume was on Evan's lapel, or, at least, I was going with that assumption. Forensics would still have to match the fibers to make sure. But then Scottie's recall of the two men clashing shoulders during rehearsal was a suitable explanation for how the beard hair got stuck on the lapel. I put a big question mark over the box with Danny's name because there were just too many holes to fill.

I wrote Joanna Fritz in box two. She was a jilted fiancée who was left holding the bill for the cancelled wedding. Plenty of motive but then there didn't seem to be a shortage of those with the way Evan ran his professional and personal life. She wasn't part of the crew, yet she happened to be nearby when the tent corner broke free. She also didn't let on to Jackson that Evan had broken off the engagement. She'd made no mention of it the night of the murder. And she was alone at the Nativity scene, giving her a weak alibi for her whereabouts during the murder. Then there was the single piece of straw I'd discovered on my search around the tent perimeter. The entire Nativity scene was filled with mounds of straw.

I drew out a third box and wrote in Tim Barton. He was on hand when the tent broke free. He was backstage during the play, and he certainly disliked his greedy, mean boss. But that was where the threads ended. There just wasn't much evidence pointing to Tim as the killer.

I sat back and looked over my primitive graph. Nothing stood out. I couldn't think of which way to turn or who to interview next to move the investigation along. I decided to get my mind off the case. Sometimes brilliant nuggets came to me when I was concentrating on something else. I grabbed my purse. I had a sulking ghost at the inn, and I promised him I'd find out about his child. A trip to the records office and my favorite slow motion records clerk would help take my mind off murder.

CHAPTER 29

The drab, out of date interior of the building where the records office was located had been spruced up with some silver tinsel and giant plastic poinsettias. I took the elevator up to the third floor and stepped out. The hallway was empty. I expected the records office to be equally deserted so close to the holidays. That was a good thing because the records clerk, Orson Nettles, was the slowest human on earth. Naturally, I had no evidence to back up that claim, but that was only because I hadn't actually met all the people on earth. But Orson would have to concentrate to beat a snail in a race.

Orson was behind the counter with his shiny, bright pink cheeks and tufts of gray hair. Even lifting his face to smile and greet me took way longer than the normal person. "Miss Taylor, right?" he said, well after I'd already reached the counter.

"Yes, hello and Merry Christmas."

"Same to you. What can I get for you? I find myself mostly at my leisure today. Apparently no one needs records when Christmas is in the air."

"My good luck then. I was wondering if you had any birth certificates from the early nineteenth century." As I said it, I remembered that Angela Applegate, a paranormal researcher had mentioned that Bonnie Ross had been sent off to another state to stay with a related family, the Suffolks. "Only this birth would have happened in another state. I'm not sure which, possibly Connecticut or New York. I'm afraid all I have to go on is the birth mother's full name, Bonnie Louise Milton or Bonnie Louise Ross, her married name. I think it would have been around 1817, if that helps."

Orson reached for a piece of paper and pencil. I tapped my toes and clenched my jaw as I waited for him to complete the journey. He took just as long to write down the names and the date. Then he walked to the computer as if he was wearing iron shoes while walking on a magnetic floor.

"I have access to a national database," Orson said with a boastful tone. "But some of the older records are harder to retrieve." He pulled his keyboard out. He held his fingers over the keys. He carefully typed in the number. I could have done it faster with the tip of my nose, but I couldn't complain. Orson was always ready to help out.

He clicked around for a few minutes. His fuzzy gray brows lifted and fell several times before he finally nodded. "Here it is. State of Connecticut, Certificate and Record of Birth."

I was anxious to see the monitor, but it was turned toward Orson. He paused to pull something out of the pocket of his pants. It was a magnifying glass.

"Sometimes these old records are faded and hard to read." He lowered his face to the monitor and lifted the magnifying glass, a feat that took him a painfully long time. By the time he positioned his eye behind the glass, I was practically chewing through the fillings in my teeth.

"Is the mother Bonnie Milton?" I asked, impatiently gripping the counter as if I could somehow pull the computer monitor my direction.

Orson's eye looked giant as he stared through the glass. "Yes, yes. Bonnie Louise Milton is listed as the mother." He straightened and lowered the magnifier. "There's no father listed."

"Oh really?" I feigned surprise. It would make sense since the baby was born out of wedlock. To avoid a family scandal there would be no mention of the baby's father. I was feeling jittery with excitement as if I'd just downed a double espresso.

"I don't suppose I'm allowed to see your monitor? Some kind of rule or something?" I asked.

He blinked at me from under his thick, expressive brows. "No rule. I'll turn it your direction. Let me just move some of this stuff." He reached for a pen and sticky note pad. Wanting to be out of the records office before the new year rang in, I helped him out by moving a stapler, a note pad and a container of paperclips.

He shifted the monitor as if he was moving a fragile piece of priceless pottery. The document was old and faded. It had been scanned into the computer, which made it even harder to read. But a name was printed clearly across the top next to the words *Name of Child*.

James Henry Milton was born on the third of October, 1817 to Bonnie Louise Milton. I was sure I wouldn't forget the name, but I was so excited about discovering that Edward had fathered a baby boy, I decided to write it down just in case.

"I could print the page for you," Orson suggested as he noticed me write down the name.

"Could you? I hate to be a bother but that would be great." I knew darn well that the printer was in the back room, and it would take an extra fifteen minutes of the day for Orson to finish the simple printing task but it would be worth the wait.

I wasn't sure how Edward would react to the news. In fact, the whole thing made me nervous as heck, but he had to know. It might be a first step on figuring out why Edward hadn't moved on to a better eternity. Preferably one where Ursula and Henry weren't arguing and hammering all day.

Orson clicked the mouse. "There we go. I'll just run and fetch the copy from the printer."

I held back my smile as I watched Orson's idea of a *run*.

CHAPTER 30

*T*he festival was buzzing with activity in the late afternoon as I walked through one last time hoping something important would jump out at me. I had so little for my article that I was fretting I wouldn't have anything in by the deadline. My lack of an article was helping to keep me out of the office. Friday afternoon meant Parker would be asking for a rough draft or an outline of what I was working on. I had no outline, no paragraphs, not even a leading sentence.

The clouds above signaled some snowfall was on its way, but that didn't stop people from browsing through the craft kiosks and sampling the various goodies being sold along the street. People were dressed in their Victorian bonnets, top hats, crinoline skirts and frock coats for the Friday evening festivities. For most people, the disastrous play was already behind them, and they were looking forward to the holiday.

I glanced across the street where the two mounted police were standing talking to a group of people who had stopped to admire the horses. I hadn't noticed that Ursula and Henry were standing with the group nibbling mincemeat pies until Ursula's distinctive voice chirped through the air.

I considered scooting past and not stopping to talk to them. My mind was wrapped in the investigation, my zero word article and the emotional information I had for my moody ghost. But Henry spotted me slinking past on the opposite side of the street. Considering I was one of the few people not wearing some kind of Victorian holiday garb, I stood out like the bah humbugger I was.

"Sunni, have you tried the mincemeat pies?" Henry held up the last piece of his pie. "Very tasty." He waved me over. I had no choice except to join them. Oddly enough, Ursula was avoiding eye contact with me. It was totally out of character. Henry motioned with his head for her to follow him as they stepped away from the horse admirers. We met a few feet away from the activity. Ursula pretended to pick at her pie crust. Ursula was one of those people who wore her feelings right out for everyone to see, and it was easy to see she was upset about something.

"Is something the matter?" I directed my question to Henry, since Ursula still hadn't lifted her face to look at me.

Henry fidgeted with his napkin and wiped his chin a few times before jamming the used napkin into his pocket. "There was a little incident at the house today," he said haltingly.

My heart dropped straight to my feet. It had to have been something big if Ursula was staying silent, letting Henry do the talking. I surveyed both of them for bandages or bruises. "Did someone get hurt?"

"No, no, it wasn't that."

His words didn't slow the worried pulse that was racing through me. If it wasn't an injury, then it had something to do with Edward.

Henry's expression slumped, and he looked genuinely upset. My mind was darting in every terrifying direction. "We do love working for you, Sunni. And the inn is the project of a lifetime."

All I could see was the top of Ursula's head and her pouty lips as she stared down at her feet to avoid eye contact.

"Henry, please, I'm about to break into a million pieces here. What on earth is going on?" I pleaded.

Henry looked at Ursula, who was still behaving like a kid embarrassed about something she'd done. He turned back to me. "Ursula noticed a piece of the baseboard was slightly crooked, and you know how she likes to do everything just right."

"Yes, that's why all of your work is so splendid." I decided it was my opportunity to throw in a compliment, something I didn't do enough with them. I dreaded the notion of having to find another contractor for the inn. I'd grown comfortable with Henry and Ursula, and they were true craftsman. My words had helped some. Ursula lifted her face to me, but she was still uncharacteristically silent.

"The thing is—" Henry paused.

Ursula had had it with her brother's slow delivery. "I was hammering away on that baseboard," she blurted, "and someone or *something* yanked the hammer right out of my hand and threw it across the room."

I could feel the color drain from my face and pool at my feet.

Henry grabbed my arm. "Are you all right, Sunni? You look just the way Ursula looked when the hammer flew across the room. I told her it was just her butterfingers." Now that the incident had been blasted out into the open, Henry had no problem talking. "I mean there wasn't anyone else in the room with us. And she was mad because I'd put the thing on crooked in the first place, so she was hammering like she was chiseling copper out of a mine."

"Yes, I'm sure that's what happened. Nothing else makes sense," I said weakly. The surrounding landscape had stopped swaying, but I was still feeling lightheaded.

Ursula shook her head. "It wasn't butterfingers. I was holding that hammer just fine." She straightened her posture. "The thing is,

165

I don't think I can work at the inn anymore." She held her chin up to show resolve, but her eyes glassed with tears.

It felt as if the dentist had dropped the lead x-ray blanket on my chest. "I would be devastated if you two left the project. Please reconsider, Ursula. Maybe you were just tired and the handle slipped." I knew my attempts at a reasonable explanation were outlandish. Someone like Ursula, who wielded a hammer like I wielded a pen, would certainly know if someone wrenched the tool from her grasp. And that *someone* was going to get a stern talking to as soon as I got home.

Henry patted my arm. "The holiday is just around the corner. We'll take the rest of the time off until after New Years. This whole thing will pass by then, and we'll be right back at it."

"I'm sure of it. You've both been working too hard. A little rest is all that's needed." My words sounded hollow, but this was the last thing I'd expected to hear when I crossed the street to talk to Henry and Ursula.

"Yes, I'm sure you're right, Sunni," Henry said with just as little conviction.

"The break will be nice for all of us." I took hold of Ursula's hands and squeezed them. "You two are the only people I trust with the restoration project."

Ursula forced a smile, then it fell instantly to a frown. "Just you be careful in that house, Sunni. Something's not right there."

"I'm perfectly safe. I admit there are occasional occurrences that are hard to explain." Before I could continue, Ursula burst forth with her own explanation.

"It's that Cider Ridge ghost. He's real," she insisted and said loud enough to gather some attention from people standing nearby. I smiled politely at them and turned back to Henry and Ursula.

I leaned closer, deciding on a new tactic. "You might be right," I whispered. "But it makes the inn that much more exciting, don't you think?" I winked. "I'll keep my eye out for anything strange and let him know he's not to mess with your tools anymore." I shrugged. "I don't have Raine's talent, but who knows, maybe he'll listen to the mistress of the house."

Henry chuckled and shook his head. "And here I was thinking that Sunni was too no-nonsense of a girl to believe in ghosts."

"I'm learning quickly that it's not any fun to be a no-nonsense girl." I winked at him. "I've got to go. I've got an article that unfortunately won't write itself."

"See you later, Sunni," Henry said cheerfully. Ursula was still quiet. She had been severely shaken by the hammer incident. Edward was going to get an earful from me about it. I just wondered what I should drop first, the stern lecture or the news that he was a dad.

With one more thing now floating in my head, I was still not ready to return to my work computer. I took a long walk around the festival and found myself at the last parking lot where some of the vendors had parked their trucks. A temporary shelter and corral had been set up for the carriage horses. One lone horse stood in the small enclosure looking bored. He paced along the front edge of the corral, snorting and pawing at the straw. The straw.

I headed across the mostly vacant lot and felt guilty that I was visiting without any kind of treat. The horse's nostrils flared. Its head lifted, and its black velvety ears turned my direction with interest. Off to the side of the temporary corral, someone had piled two bales of hay. It was mostly covered with a blue vinyl tarp. I glanced around and decided it wouldn't hurt to snatch a few pieces of hay so as not to show up empty handed.

The horse gladly accepted my meager offering. His head stayed straight up as his muzzle swished side to side, slowly chewing the hay. I patted his neck and rubbed behind his ear, a favorite spot for Butterscotch, Emily's Belgian mare. It seemed to be this horse's favorite spot too. The animal tilted his big head so I could reach his ears with ease.

Some of the bedding, the thick yellow straw, had drifted out below the bottom rung of the corral. I patted my new friend's neck a few times and then bent down to pick up a piece of the straw. I didn't know much about straw, but it seemed to be the exact same material that Joanna had used in the manger. It also matched the piece of straw I found near the tent. I looked back across town, over the many heads, bonnets and top hats, to the corner where the tent once stood. The Nativity scene was in between, off a side street. It seemed more and more likely that the straw I found had nothing at all to do with the murder and everything to do with the direction of the wind. That meant I was even further behind in solving Evan's murder than when I started.

I headed back to the newspaper office. There was little chance of me getting any words on paper this afternoon, particularly after the stressful conversation I'd just had with Henry and Ursula. I would go home, make myself a big cup of cocoa and decide which blow to hit Edward with first.

CHAPTER 31

*T*he house was quiet. I was relieved. I sat at the kitchen table staring out at the light snow that had started to fall and cradled my cup of cocoa. It wouldn't take much for me to find Edward, usually just a few calls into the air and he'd materialize on one of his favorite perches. But I needed some time to myself first. His noticeable absence meant he was possibly brooding somewhere, wherever it was he went when he vanished. It could also mean that he knew he'd done something bad today and that I'd probably heard about it from Ursula.

I finished the last of the mini marshmallows in my cup and was just about to toss a few more in when a cold vapor crossed over me. Edward appeared in the chair across from me. "I suppose that irritating woman told you what happened."

I stared at him across the table. It always amazed me how many emotions could be expressed on a transparent face. "Yes, I heard all about it." I leaned back on my chair. The cocoa and time alone had calmed my nerves some. "If I don't repair this old inn, it will most likely be torn down. We've discussed this before. Your world is the inside of the house and the front porch. What do you think will happen to you when this all disappears?" I circled my arms around the kitchen. "You are stuck in this middle eternity, but what if it is wiped away? Have you given that big question any thought?"

Edward's image faded away and reappeared on the hearth, his favorite spot.

"That hearth would go right along with the house," I added as I stood up and walked toward him. "I don't say this to upset you. I say it to let you know that you need this house, but if it's falling down around us, then neither of us will have a place to live. Well, exist. You get the picture. And fixing this house will take a lot of hammering and sawing and construction noise, no matter who is wielding the tools."

Edward's long, white fingers curled around his loosened cravat. He hung onto it like someone holding onto the edges of a towel around their neck. "That woman is vexatious. That woman with a hammer is extra unbearable."

Something suddenly occurred to me. I crossed my arms and stared up at him. "It bothers you to see a woman wearing overalls and slinging tools around."

"She can do whatever she wants," he said curtly. "But it is ridiculous for a woman to hold nails between her lips and saw wood in two."

I shook my head. "I'm a numbskull. Why didn't I think of this before? Your beliefs and opinions are still stuck back in the early nineteenth century."

"A much finer and more respectable time to live, obviously," he said.

"Yes, you were quite the model of respectability back then." It was a remark that would have been better left unsaid. Edward vanished, but I knew he was still lingering.

I carried my cup to the sink and kept talking to the empty room, knowing full well a certain pair of ears would hear every word. "What you did today was dangerous, Edward. You want me to keep your existence a secret, then you do something that can't be explained away by a sudden gust of wind or a dog." I finished rinsing my cup and put it in the rack. "It makes me worry that you are not just a lost spirit but a malicious one."

His image popped up right next to me. His unexpected popping in and out didn't startle me anymore. "What is this word, malicious? It doesn't sound nice."

"No, it's the opposite of nice. But you yanked a hammer from Ursula's hand and threw it across the room. Someone could have been hurt. Do I need to worry about you?" Deep down, I didn't feel the least bit threatened by Edward's presence, but I knew this line of questioning would bother him. Hopefully, it would make him think twice before pulling such a terrible stunt again.

He came close enough that I could feel the cool cloud atmosphere circling around him. "I would never hurt you, Sunni. Surely, you know that." His tone was so contrite and distressed it made me feel a twinge of guilt.

I smiled at him. "I know that, Edward, but what happened today—that can never happen again. I can't keep your secret if you make such a bold misstep."

His face dropped, and he coasted back to the comfort of his safe perch on the hearth. He looked truly sorry about it all. And now I had another zinger to throw out at him. I briefly considered holding the information back but decided just to go for it.

"Edward, you had a son. James Henry Milton was born on the third of October, 1817."

His expression shifted from disbelief to an emotion I'd never seen before on his face. "Are you certain?"

"Of course since I wasn't there I can never be certain, but I found a birth certificate. I have it if you want to see it. All the details and the time period match up. Bonnie had a baby boy. *Your baby boy.*"

He dropped down from the hearth and paced, or at least his version of pacing where feet never touched the floor. "I have a son."

A knock on the door startled both of us out of the intense moment. Edward vanished. I caught my breath as I headed to the door. Whoever it was, they had terrible timing. The last thing I wanted was to drop the news on Edward and then leave him on his own.

Redford and Newman came charging up behind me as if they were ready to offer protection if needed. Only I knew what they really wanted was to be social. I peeked through the small window on the front door. It was Jackson.

I opened the door. "Jackson," I said still slightly out of breath.

He pulled his hand out from behind his back. He was holding a tiny Christmas tree decorated in foil wrapped chocolates and candy canes. "I thought since you didn't have time to put up a tree, I'd bring you one."

My mind was still on Edward, but I forced a smile. "Yes, great, a tree. I'll have no choice but to get in the spirit with a cute little tree in the house." My words sounded stilted, but I couldn't help it.

Jackson's own brilliant smile dimmed considerably. "Maybe I shouldn't have forced the tree on you. And I should have texted. I'm interrupting your evening." He turned to leave, but I grabbed his hand.

"No, you're not interrupting." I took hold of the tree. "I love it. Will it be considered bad manners if I end up eating all the decorations before Santa shows up?"

He smiled lightly. I was not myself when I answered the door and he sensed it. I stepped into the kitchen first and sucked in a sharp breath when I found Edward hovering in front of the kitchen window, staring out at the snowfall. I cleared my throat loudly and tilted my head asking him to disappear but only Jackson noticed.

"Everything all right, Sunni?" It was rare to hear Jackson call me by my real name.

"Everything's fine." I placed the tree in the center of my kitchen table and reached up to rub my neck. "Just a little kink from sitting at the computer all day." Not that I'd actually sat at the computer all day or even for more than an hour.

My gaze flicked back to the window. Edward was gone. He reappeared right behind Jackson with a glower that made me swallow hard. I attempted an imperceptible head shake to let my ghost know he needed to back off, but I quickly discovered nothing is imperceptible to a highly skilled detective.

"I should go," Jackson said. "I just wanted to drop off the tree."

"No, no don't go," I said far too abruptly, making the whole thing even more awkward. Edward wasn't leaving. I'd told him something explosive, and it was obvious that he needed to talk more about it. I rubbed my head. "You know, Jackson, I sort of have a headache."

"Yep, got it," he said rather coldly. "Sorry to just drop by. I won't do it again." He turned sharply. I held my breath as he walked right through Edward's image. He stopped and turned his head slightly to look back at the space he'd just passed. Whatever he felt, he shook it off in his rush to get out of my house.

I hurried after him. "Jackson, I love the tree. I do. It's just I'm—" I fell silent. How could I possibly have ended my explanation? I'm sorry but I have to provide some much needed one on one with my resident ghost who just learned he was a father? My heart felt like stone as I watched Jackson open the door.

"I'll see you later, Sunni." His footsteps pounded the porch steps as he raced down them.

"Jackson, I'm sorry. I'll talk to you tomorrow, all right?"

He didn't answer. I watched from the front door as he climbed into his car and drove away. My throat ached as I shut the door. I'd just blown it big time. I'd been trying to convince myself that a relationship with Jackson was the last thing I needed, but in truth, I wanted it. I really, really wanted it.

CHAPTER 32

*I*t turned out Edward wanted mostly to sulk alone. He sat like a depressed gargoyle on the kitchen hearth while I stared at the sweet, little tree on my table. That was the end of it. I could sense the doom of a fresh new relationship as Jackson climbed into his car and drove off.

"You're sad," Edward said from his perch.

"Looks like we're both a couple of grim gussies tonight," I said lightly.

"I didn't mean to scare him away, but he takes a lot for granted always showing up here unannounced. In my day—" He started but stopped when I put up my hand.

"For the millionth time, this is not *your day*. In fact, *your day* is so far back in time, we call it history."

Edward pretended to brush invisible dust off his breeches. "I doubt you've actually said it a million times. That would be an extraordinary amount."

"Figure of speech. I was trying to convey that I've said it over and over, and you have ignored it over and over. And, yes, you scared him away, but I'm sure you won't have to worry about him showing up anymore because this time you or, I should say *we,* chased him off for good."

"Then he is a fool if he is giving up so easily on someone of your character."

I smiled at him over my tiny tree. "Thank you, Edward. That's nice of you to say."

He nodded politely. "Do you think he survived?" Edward lifted his face and looked at me. "Do you think little James survived infanthood, or, for that matter, childhood?"

"I don't know for sure, but I can find out. I've got a contact for an elderly woman in Connecticut who knew something about Bonnie. It was her ancestors who took care of Bonnie when Cleveland sent her away." A yawn overtook me. "Excuse me. I'm pooped." I got up from the table. "I'm heading to bed." I just needed to say the word and Redford and Newman pushed up from their kitchen pillows and plodded down the hall to the bedroom.

"I'm glad I know now," Edward said before I disappeared down the hallway.

I peered around the doorway at him.

"I'm glad I know about my son. Thank you. And—you're too good for that wild haired man."

"You could have left it at thank you, but that's all right. Like I said, you won't be seeing him again."

CHAPTER 33

*a*s tired as I was from the day, once I got into bed, I found my mind wouldn't rest. I walked to the dresser and picked up my laptop. I propped up my pillows against the headboard and sat in bed with my computer. I needed to get Jackson out of my head and decided to focus on the investigation.

After drawing out the diagram of the victim surrounded by the possible suspects and motives, I wasn't getting a strong sense from any of them. I was still leaning toward Danny, mostly because he gained the most from Evan's death. Still, it was hard to pin the label cold blooded killer on the man. He seemed far too kind and reasonable. But then I only knew him from a few casual chats. It was entirely possible there was a sinister, dark side to his character that he was great at hiding. How many times had I seen a news crew interview a killer's neighbor and friend just to hear them say, 'I had no idea. He was the nicest person. Always friendly'.

After piecing together my modern version of *A Christmas Carol*, one with a much more tragic ending, it seemed I had the important characters. But what about John Marlin, Evan's late partner?

What were the circumstances of his death? I needed something to occupy my mind and hopefully make me sleepy, so I typed in the name along with Evan Weezer.

There were multiple entries. It seemed ten years ago, John and Evan were up and coming stars in the commercial real estate business. They'd worked on small projects, office spaces and industrial buildings for several years, but the sale that put them on the map was a massive multimillion dollar deal where a developer bought up an entire block of old stores to build a shopping mall. The pair must have made a fortune in commission on the deal.

I moved on to the next article that discussed John Marlin's untimely death. "Commercial real estate agent, John Marlin, was discovered dead in his bed at Jollyside Hotel. The coroner marked it as death by natural causes. Marlin and his business partner, Evan Weezer, were in town to finish up the last minute contract details on the future shopping mall in the center of town. His death did not impact the finalization of the deal, and the shopping mall will go on as planned."

Apparently, Evan wasn't too broken up about Marlin's unexpected death to put those finishing touches on the contract. The deal was not delayed and everything went through as planned, including the large commission, a commission Evan no longer had to share.

The next entry mentioned something about a lawsuit. I clicked on it and read the first line. "Aurora Marlin, widow of John Marlin, sues Evan Weezer for a commission that belonged to her late husband." I sat up so suddenly the laptop slipped off the fuzzy blanket covering my legs. I pushed it back into place and read the line again. How many Aurora's could there be in the area? I scrolled down and found a small, grainy picture that may or may not have been the woman running the festival's carriage ride. But my opinion was falling firmly in the positive match section when the article mentioned that Aurora Marlin was an accomplished equestrian and horse breeder. As I predicted, the lawsuit had to do with the last deal John made before his death. The judge ruled in Weezer's favor, cutting Aurora out of a large sum of money. Aurora Marlin also insinuated that her husband's death should have been investigated. Obviously angry and upset, she even suggested that the coroner was being paid off by Evan to say that John died naturally, in his sleep. According to her, Marlin had been in excellent health and was very fit. It did seem rather strange that a fit, healthy man would die in his sleep and right before he was about to get very rich on a business deal.

I sat back with a sigh. Had there been another suspect all along? I glanced at my phone on the nightstand. Under any other circumstance, I would have picked it up and quickly texted Jackson with the news. But something told me he didn't want to hear from me tonight. I couldn't face him not texting back. Chances were, his research team was already delving into the partnership and subsequent lawsuit. But did they realize that Aurora Marlin had been in town for the festival?

I reached toward the phone and then pulled my hand back. "Let him do his job and you do yours," I muttered to myself. And my job was to get a good story. It seemed I might just have stumbled onto one.

I closed my eyes and tried to picture the audience and the stage that night. I couldn't be positive but I didn't remember seeing Aurora anywhere in the crowd. That would make sense because she was busy with her carriage rides. However, her schedule might have allowed her to take a long enough break to stab the man who stole money she thought belonged to her. I would have been angry too. A decent partner would have sent John's half to his grieving wife, but nothing about Evan Weezer seemed decent. The only evidence I had placing Aurora at the scene of the crime was a single strand of straw, but that could have been carried in by the wind or even on someone else's clothing.

Another yawn took off in full glory before I could even cover my mouth. This new information had taken my mind off my troubles for the night. With any luck, I'd sleep well. I needed to get an early start in the morning. Tomorrow was the last day of the festival. Aurora would be packing up her horses and carriage and leaving town. I needed to strike up a conversation with her. The best way I knew how was to take a carriage ride through town. I had been daydreaming about a romantic carriage ride, preferably with a tall, handsome detective sitting next to me, but it seemed this ride, I'd be going it alone. Oh well, I was an independent woman who didn't need to depend on a man, even a particularly appealing man, to be happy. And if I solved the murder before him, all the better.

CHAPTER 34

I'd overslept and found myself rushing around to get dressed and out the door. It was strange starting the morning without Ursula and Henry. By now they would have been fighting over the toaster and the last cup of coffee in the pot. I hoped they planned to return, but for now, I couldn't worry about it. I had a murder to solve. I just wasn't sure how yet.

I was almost clear of the house when Lana's truck pulled up to the inn, only Chris was driving it. Mom climbed out with a big smile and her arms ready for a hug. The amber brooch dangled from her sweater.

"Sunni, you'll never guess my big news," she chirped as she ran toward me. Her arms went around me for a super tight hug.

"I know all about the amber brooch," I grunted through the hug. Her arms tightened more. It seemed her Woman's Club exercise class was doing its job.

"Isn't it stunning?" She released me and lifted the brooch without taking it off the sweater. "He had it hiding behind my dinner plate last night." Her smile nearly split her face in two, and her eyes sparkled like a little girl who'd just been told she was actually a princess of a distant country. Or at least that was the thing that would make my eyes glisten the way hers were shining. Even for my mom, it seemed an oddly, over the top reaction to a brooch.

Chris reached us. Mom quickly turned to him with a finger to her lips, silencing him. "I haven't told her yet," Mom said. She faced me again with eyes still sparkling. "It's cold outside. Let's go in and have some coffee. I have some news to tell you."

News to tell me. I'd been thickheaded or maybe that was on purpose. My gaze dropped instinctively to her left hand and there it was—the news yet untold. Mom was wearing a diamond engagement ring. She'd removed the single gold wedding band she'd been wearing all my life. I'd only ever seen her without it when she was stuffing the turkey at Thanksgiving. Even then, it always sat nearby on a cup saucer waiting to return to its rightful place on her hand.

I was stunned into a sort of trance. I turned toward the porch. The three of us headed inside and to the kitchen. During the journey, I was trying to process how I felt about the news she hadn't told me yet but that was standing out like a black and white headline on her ring finger.

I'd turned off the coffee pot on my way out, but it was still hot. Without asking, I poured them both a cup and carried the coffee to the table where they'd sat down. The day before, Lana had given Mom and Chris a short tour of the work that had been done on the inn. I'd been at work, so Mom hadn't sat in my kitchen yet.

"I would love to have a huge kitchen like this." She smiled sweetly. "I don't suppose it's made you want to cook more?" she asked.

"I suppose not," I said almost curtly.

Mom tugged at one of the candy ornaments on the tree Jackson brought. Seeing the little spruce first thing this morning had made me replay the entire short visit in my head over and over until I had to force myself not to think of it.

"Maggie, I think we just stopped Sunni on her way to work. Maybe this can wait," Chris suggested. The man hardly knew me, but he could sense my tension, even if the woman who gave birth to me could not.

Mom waved her ringed finger. "Surely, she can spare a few minutes for something life changing."

I took hold of her fluttery fingers and did my best to admire the ring. It was far more flashy than her other jewelry.

"I guess congratulations are in order." A small noise hauled my attention away from the ring. I held my breath for a second, hoping that Edward wouldn't make an appearance. He would only add to the mix of my topsy turvy morning.

I did my best to look happy. Chris saw right through the act, but Mom twittered on with talk of a possible date next spring and where they would eventually live. Maybe I wasn't giving Chris enough credit for being a genuinely decent guy.

Without warning, he reached across the table and placed his hand over mine. I hadn't taken the time yet to notice that he had very kind hazel eyes. "I know you were very close with your dad. He sounds like a wonderful man. Please know that I'm not here to replace him in any way. I love your Mom, and I want to live the rest of my life with her."

His words tugged deep down in my chest. I was feeling like a heel for being so negative about their relationship. "I'm happy for you both." I looked at each of them. "I really am."

Chris tapped the table. "Well, Maggie, we need to let this reporter get to work. The news waits for no one, not even past their prime couples."

"Who are you calling past her prime?" Mom said with a chin lift and then laughed. "Who am I kidding? Chris is right. We just wanted to tell you the news ourselves before Lana spilled it. You know how your sister likes to be at the front of the line on everything."

"I know it too well." We stood up from the table and walked them out to their car. I locked up so I could leave as well. I was anxious to follow my new lead on Aurora Marlin.

"Emily's making dinner tonight," Mom said as they reached the car. "You should invite that handsome young detective."

The mere mention of Jackson took some of the steam out of my engine. "I'm sure he's busy, but I'll be there. I'll see you two later."

CHAPTER 35

*W*ith today being the last day of the festival, there were few parking spots left. I parked near the newspaper office, a good mile from the festival. It was Saturday so the newspaper was closed, but a light was on in Parker's office. I lifted the collar of my coat and tried to slink past the windows unnoticed. I wasn't two feet past the building when Parker bellowed my name.

"Taylor, get in here. I haven't seen anything from you all week."

I temporarily considered pretending that I didn't hear him, knowing full well he wouldn't follow on foot, but his voice was like thunder.

I swung around and walked back to him. "Hey, boss, why are you working on a Saturday?" I thought a topic switch might help, especially because the man always enjoyed when *he* was the topic.

"Wife's got some cookie exchange party happening. I needed to get out. What are you writing about since the play was a disaster?"

I patted my pocket where my notebook was cradled. "You know me, Parker. I'm hot on the trail of something big. In fact, I was just heading to the festival where I'm hoping to find out some intriguing details about the murder."

His crooked moustache rocked back and forth. "I'll need something Monday."

I gave him a thumbs up, one of his favorite gestures. "Prepare to be amazed," I said cheerily. My smile faded the second I turned around. I didn't have one word of the article done, but with any luck, my visit to the festival was going to change that.

Nerves were bouncing around in my stomach like fireflies when I reached the place where Aurora was selling tickets for her Victorian carriage ride through town. She was an attractive forty-something woman with the tanned, fit look of someone who spent a lot of time outdoors. Her carriage was stopped along the curbside. Both horses looked asleep behind their blinders with their heads drooped low and the bells on their bridles silent. Aurora was talking to the two mounted police. They seemed to be discussing the saddles on the police horses and nothing of a serious nature.

I took a deep breath and headed toward her. I'd contemplated different ways of introducing myself but ended up with the standard announcement about being a reporter with the *Junction Times*. Any other way seemed underhanded. It was better she knew exactly who I was, even if it meant her answers were less forthcoming. Occasionally, the press pass worked the opposite way and caused people to spill everything they had on their mind. I had absolutely no evidence that Aurora had anything to do with Evan's death, but she was in town for the festival and it seemed she had a good motive.

"Hello." I pulled out my press pass. "I'm Sunni Taylor with the *Junction Times*. I'm doing an article on the festival, (which was at least partially true) and I was hoping to take a ride on your beautiful carriage." I tapped my chin. "Now, does a tall, dapper Englishman in top hat and tails come with the ticket purchase?" I'd found early on in my career that humor always helped break the ice.

Aurora laughed. "I'm sorry to disappoint you. But I can guarantee a nice ride through town."

I pulled out the ten dollars it took for a ticket. "Carriage ride for one then, and I'll just imagine the dapper man sitting next to me."

Aurora took the money and showed me to the carriage. She opened the small black lacquer door and folded out two steps. I climbed up and sat down on the velvet cushions. It was rather exciting. I almost wished I wasn't there to pry information out of her.

Aurora shut the door of the open carriage and walked to the front to adjust the various straps on the horses. I leaned my arm along the edge and hung my head out to strike up a conversation. "My article was supposed to be about the Dickens' play, but I'm sure you heard how that went."

She nodded but didn't say anything in response. She'd unbuckled a harness and had decided to move it a notch higher. She was concentrating on her task when I tossed out a question. "Were you at the play? It was truly horrifying."

"No, I was working the carriage rides." Her earlier demeanor had darkened some.

Naturally, the sudden glacial chill around her didn't stop me. "I heard that Evan Weezer used to be partners with your husband."

She pulled the strap on the horse's bridle just a little harder than she or the horse had expected. The animal lifted its head in protest and she loosened it.

"Yes, that's true, but I have nothing to do with Weezer's business anymore," she said sharply. I'd hit a nerve.

"I don't like speaking badly about the dead, but from what I gathered in my interviews, Evan Weezer didn't have many friends. Let's just say he wasn't the nicest person in town." I tried to keep my tone airy. What I hoped was that Aurora would chime in about her feelings toward Evan. She couldn't think too highly of the man after losing a great deal of money to him.

But Aurora held her mouth in a firm line. She finally glanced my direction with an unfriendly expression. "Is this some sort of interview?"

"What? No, I'm just trying to get a good picture of Weezer for the article."

Her face snapped my direction as she checked another piece of tack. "I thought it was about the festival."

"Yes, yes, it is, but it would be hard to write an article about the festival and not mention the murder. Don't you think?"

She shook her head. "I don't know. I'm not a journalist."

I rested back and tried to organize my thoughts before asking another question. I was losing her fast. She seemed to grow angrier with each question. I decided to hold back until we took off or risk having her ask me to leave the carriage.

I waited for her to finish checking the horses. I glanced out at the people milling about the festival buying goodies and last minute gifts. My gaze swept across the mostly unfamiliar faces and landed directly on one very familiar one.

Jackson was a good two blocks away, walking our direction. It seemed his focus was on the carriage. I couldn't tell if he was looking at me or at the area in general. Either way, seeing him sent a jolt of nerves through me. Had he discovered the connection between the carriage driver and Evan Weezer? Darn him for always being one step ahead just when I was sure I was one step ahead.

Aurora walked up to the driver's box on the carriage. As she reached to pull herself up, the phone rang in her pocket. I sat forward with a gasp. It was *Jingle Bells*.

Aurora hadn't noticed my stunned reaction. She stopped her ascent into the carriage and pulled her phone out. She glanced at it but decided to let the call go to voicemail. That's when she noticed me staring at her.

"*Jingle Bells*," I said on a stunned breath.

"Yes, it's my favorite," she said with a shrug, unsure why I would be so shocked.

"You were at the play that night. When Evan fell dead, I hurried up on stage to help. I heard the ringtone behind the tent."

Her face blanched as white as the snow covered sidewalk behind her. "I don't know what you're talking about."

"It was you." I hadn't meant to say the words out loud but they dribbled from my lips.

Aurora's face hardened as she pulled her whip from the driver's seat. Her arm came up and the whip cracked the air over the heads of the horses. They lurched forward with loud whinnies and took off at a full gallop.

A scream was knocked out of me as I was thrown back hard against the seat.

CHAPTER 36

*T*error glued my eyes shut and my fingers clutched at the upholstery, the seat, the edge of the carriage, anything I could grab that might keep me from flying out of the open vehicle. The impossibly loud clatter of horse hooves smacking asphalt was punctuated by the screams and yells of the people standing on the sidewalks.

The carriage careened side to side. One side suddenly lifted up, signaling that two wheels had come off the ground. The jarring thud that followed as the wheels thankfully made contact with the road snapped my teeth shut hard.

I pried open my eyes and tried to think rationally over the pounding of my pulse. The festival passed by with a blur. The horrified expressions I saw as the carriage sped past assured me I was in grave danger. The horses steamed straight ahead, two frightened animals, with no one to rein them in.

My survival instincts kicked in. I threw myself across to the opposite seat and tried to peer over the front lip of the passenger compartment. The driver's box was a good foot away and at least three feet higher than the passenger seat. I got up on my knees and reached for the back of the driver's seat, hoping to heave myself over and not completely sure what to do once I got there.

I heard sirens behind me as we left the festival area and headed toward the main part of town. After several tries, my fingers grasped the edge of the driver's seat. The carriage swerved violently to the side, causing me to lose my grip. I was thrown against the side of the carriage. My head smacked the edge, and I dropped to the floor in agony. I held my head to stop the pain and dizziness.

Probably only two minutes had passed since the mad carriage ride had begun, but it felt like an eternity. The horses didn't seem to tire. If anything, the wild gallop through town only gave them more spirit. I knew we were heading for Crimson Grove, a busy road that connected Firefly Junction to Birch Highlands. So many nightmarish scenarios followed in my dazed state of mind that I shut my eyes hard to erase them.

As I opened them, I came to the dreadful conclusion that I'd hit my head hard. I was hallucinating. I'd conjured up an image of Jackson riding past, hunkered down low over a horse's neck.

My life started coming up in bits and pieces as I convinced myself this would be the end for me. Tears burned my eyes and I ducked into a ball, deciding it would be the least painful way to go if the carriage was broadsided by a car or truck.

The carriage lurched again, this time front to back, sending me rolling and ricocheting between the seats. A voice above my head said "Whoa" in a deep, dulcet tone.

The carriage seemed to slow, only I was in such a haze it was hard to tell for sure. I released the hold I had on my knees and lifted my face. Sunlight burned my eyes for a second, then a shadow fell across me, clearing my vision. A tall figure sat up on the driver's seat. His big arms working to gain control of the horses.

"Whoa, whoa, there you go."

The sound of Jackson's voice brought me instantly to tears. The carriage slowed to a mild roll, eventually creaking to a stop. The clatter of horse hooves fell silent and only the animals' panting breaths filled the air.

Jackson tied off the reins and turned sharply around on the box seat. His worried gaze found me sitting on the floor of the carriage. "Sunni, are you all right?" I had never heard him sound scared before. It made the tears fall faster.

I wiped at them with shaky hands. "I am now," I said through sobs.

Voices and footsteps rumbled behind the carriage. I pulled myself up onto the seat. My legs collapsed on the way down. Festival goers, shop owners and one of the mounted policemen stood a safe distance from the carriage, not wanting to startle the horses. I waved to the worried onlookers to let them know I was all right.

Cheers and applause rang out as Jackson climbed down from the carriage. The fear in his face had not disappeared as he opened the door. He held out his hand and gazed at me with dark amber eyes fraught with worry.

My limbs were shaking so hard, it was hard to reach for his hand. The second our palms met, he had me out of the carriage and in his arms.

"Thought I'd lost you, Bluebird," he muttered as his mouth pressed against my forehead.

I kept my face smothered against his chest, waiting to regain a few ounces of composure. His strong embrace was helping. His protective arms stayed wrapped around me. His erratic heartbeat drummed against my cheek. It was pounding nearly as fast as my own.

I finally took a steadying breath and peered up at him. But I was speechless. I still couldn't believe I was standing there, alive in his arms. "This is real, right?" My voice wavered.

He squeezed me tighter. "As real as can be. And as far as I'm concerned this is that kaboom moment." I'd barely caught my breath when his mouth came down over mine for a kiss.

The tension in my body disappeared and was immediately replaced with the warmth and giddiness that came from an extraordinary and long awaited kiss. My knees were still weak from the frightening experience. The kiss wasn't going to help them solidify any time soon.

After a long kiss and a round of cheers from what seemed to be the entire town, Jackson lifted his mouth from my lips.

"I'm definitely seeing fireworks," I smiled up at him. "Of course, that might have something to do with the blow to my head."

Jackson noticed, for the first time, the bump on the side of my head just above my temple. He touched it lightly, making me wince.

"We need to get you checked out by a doctor."

The sound of approaching horse hooves startled me. Jackson tightened his hold on me and kissed my head right above the bump. "That's just Officer Vickers." His arms lowered and we turned to watch the mounted officer walk toward us.

He climbed down and led the horse to us. "That was better than any western movie," Officer Vickers quipped. "I think you've missed your calling, Detective. You should have been a stunt man."

Jackson rubbed his lower back. "I'll be feeling it tonight. I haven't ridden on a horse in years. Guess it's like riding a bicycle. Did Officer Truro get his horse back?"

"Yes, Old Pete hasn't been ridden like that for awhile. After you jumped off of him onto the carriage he trotted right off to the nearest green patch to graze." Officer Vickers was young, late twenties at the most. His thick hair was brushed back out of the way of his riding helmet. "We've detained Aurora Marlin. She's back at the start of this wild carriage ride." Vickers nodded politely at me. "Glad to see you're all right."

I smiled weakly back at him. I hadn't released my hold on Jackson's coat yet.

"I'm going back to talk to her right now," Jackson said.

Vickers' curious gaze flicked from me to Jackson and back again.

"Is there anything else, Vickers?" Jackson asked.

"No, sir." He shook his head but then stopped. "Detective Jackson, sir," he said hesitantly. "I know you just saved her and all, and I know, well—" He shook his head again. "Never mind."

"If you're wondering, Vickers, I didn't just kiss a complete stranger." Jackson put his arm around my shoulder. "I know Miss Taylor well."

Vickers nodded. "I'm going to ride back. I've called a car for you and Miss Taylor."

A squad car arrived just seconds later. Jackson opened the back door of the car and held my hand until I was safely inside. He climbed in next to me.

I stared at the back of the officer's head through the metal screen. "I never thought I'd say this, but I'm relieved to be sitting in the back of this police car. What a morning." I looked over at him. My head was throbbing from the bump, but I was starting to feel normal again. It helped me retrieve the events of the last fifteen minutes. "You've detained Aurora Marlin? She did this on purpose. I saw the whip go up over the horses' heads. The next thing I knew I was flying through the festival in that unwieldy carriage."

Jackson turned slightly toward me. "I saw it happen. But why? Why did she want to hurt you?"

"I *might* have accused her of murder."

"Might have?"

"Yes. It's all because of *Jingle Bells*. The night of the murder, when you raced up on stage, I followed. In the midst of the chaos, I heard someone's phone go off just outside the tent. The ringtone was *Jingle Bells*. I didn't think much about it again until Aurora's phone went off. Her husband was John Marlin—"

"Evan's late business partner," Jackson finished for me. "That's why I was heading over to talk to her."

I sat back dejectedly. "So you already knew she was the killer? I thought I had you beat this time."

He took my hand. "You did have me beat, Bluebird. I was going to ask her a few questions just to find out where she was during the time of the murder. Only you've already answered that for me. A matching ringtone is pretty light evidence, but since she decided to take justice into her own hands and take out a witness right in front of everyone, she just sealed her fate."

The festival goers and vendors were cleaning up some of the chaos left behind by the runaway carriage ride through town. Fortunately, it seemed no one got hurt, including the horses.

Aurora Marlin was standing in her green velvet coat and pants looking about as distressed as a person could look. Her face was ashen white. Even her lips were pale gray.

The officer parked the squad car and got out to open the back door. Jackson took my hand again and lowered his gaze to me. "Sunni, don't scare me like that again."

"Trust me, I won't be climbing into a horse-drawn carriage anytime soon."

His brow arched. He continued to stare at me.

"And I won't accuse anyone of murder again either," I added.

He nodded. "Good idea." We climbed out of the car. One of the officers greeted us before we took a few steps. He was holding up his phone.

"Detective Jackson, you're already trending." He showed us the phone. Someone had captured video of Jackson's fast gallop through town. When he caught up to the runaway carriage, he leapt from the saddle onto the driver's seat.

I peered up at him. "You risked your life." My voice wavered again.

He placed his palm against my cheek and leaned forward to kiss my forehead. "I needed to save my little Bluebird."

CHAPTER 37

*I*t was the perfect way to spend the day after Christmas. Mom and Chris sat on the tailgate of Lana's truck sipping hot coffee from a thermos as the 'kids' sledded down the hill behind the inn.

Jackson had booked Aurora Marlin for murder and for attempted murder, which meant I would be involved in a court case. I wasn't thrilled about it, but the woman gave me the fright of my life. If Jackson hadn't stopped the carriage before the horses pulled me into traffic, I was sure I would have died. Naturally, Jackson's bravery had won a solid gold place in my family's heart now. He'd landed pretty solidly in mine too.

"I'll race you," Jackson said as he shoved the bottom edge of his sled into the snow like a surfboard in sand.

"What does the winner get?" I asked, always intrigued by a challenge.

"Dinner?" he said.

I crinkled my nose. "Kind of boring."

"How about a cuddle in front of the fireplace, loser brings the cocoa and marshmallows."

"You're on." I positioned the sled in front of me. Lana, Raine, Emily and Nick stood on the sidelines to watch.

"That section there right by the sapling is really icy," Nick called to Jackson. "It'll give you the advantage."

I put a hand on my hip. "Thank you, traitorous brother-in-law."

Nick lifted his hands. "We men have to stick to together when manly honor is at stake."

We lowered our sleds. I shot him a sideways glance. "I want the jumbo marshmallows. None of those puny ones."

Lana said ready, set, go. I dove belly first onto the sled. Jackson took off just a little after. His weight helped him catch up quickly. "No fair, gravity is on your side," I yelled.

"Yeah but you've got less wind resistance." He lowered his head.

My sled hit several bumps, sending me airborne twice and managing to knock the breath from me on each landing.

Jackson glided past, and I grabbed his ankle. He looked back. "Hey, no tailgaters," he laughed.

He tried to shake me loose but ended up flipping his sled. I didn't react in time and forgot to let go of his ankle. I flew off my sled and landed in the snow, face to face and directly on top of him.

"This plan worked perfectly," he said. He reached up and took hold of my head to bring my lips down to his.

Nick whistled loudly as we kissed.

I climbed off of him and offered him a hand to yank him from his bed of snow.

He hopped to his feet and his arm went around me. He wiped a piece of snow off my nose.

"I think I won by default," I said.

"You cheated," he said.

"Now you know I'm *that* kind of girl."

He held me tighter. "Oh yeah, what kind of girl is that?"

"One who will stop at nothing to get her cocoa and marsh-mallows."

We easily ignored the teasing jeers and whistles from my family as we stood in the snow and kissed.

ABOUT THE AUTHOR

London Lovett is the author of the Firefly Junction and Port Danby Cozy Mystery series. She loves getting caught up in a good mystery and baking delicious new treats!

Subscribe to London's newsletter [londonlovett.com] to never miss an update.

You can also join London for fun discussions, giveaways and more in her *Secret Sleuths* Facebook group.

https://www.facebook.com/groups/londonlovettssecretsleuths/

Instagram @LondonLovettWrites

https://www.londonlovett.com/
londonlovettwrites@gmail.com

Printed in Great Britain
by Amazon

41536780R00118